Walpurgis Night,
or the Steps of
the Commander

Walpurgis Night, or the Steps of the Commander

A Tragicomedy in Five Acts

VENEDIKT EROFEEV

TRANSLATED BY MARIAN SCHWARTZ

WITH AN INTRODUCTION BY KAREN RYAN

YALE UNIVERSITY PRESS ■ NEW HAVEN & LONDON

A MARGELLOS
WORLD REPUBLIC OF LETTERS BOOK

Yale University Press books may be purchased in quantity for educational, business, or promotional use. For information, please e-mail sales.press@yale.edu (U.S. office) or sales@yaleup.co.uk (U.K. office).

Set in Electra and Nobel type by Tseng Information Systems, Inc.

Printed in the United States of America.

Library of Congress Cataloging-in-Publication Data
Erofeev, Venedikt, 1938–1990, author.
[Val'purgieva noch'. English]
Walpurgis night, or The steps of the commander / Venedikt Erofeev ; translated by Marian Schwartz, with an introduction by Karen Ryan.
pages ; cm. — (Margellos world republic of letters)
ISBN 978-0-300-15986-8 (pbk : alk. paper)
I. Schwartz, Marian, translator. II. Ryan, Karen L., 1958– writer of added commentary. III. Title. IV. Title: Walpurgis night. V. Title: Steps of the commander. VI. Series: Margellos world republic of letters book.
PG3479.7.R59V3513 2014
891.72'44—dc23
                                                                              2013046031

A catalogue record for this book is available from the British Library.

This paper meets the requirements of ANSI/NISO Z39.48–1992 (Permanence of Paper).

10 9 8 7 6 5 4 3 2 1

CONTENTS

INTRODUCTION

Venedikt Erofeev's reputation is largely based on a single work, the brilliant prose poem *Moscow to the End of the Line* (*Moskva-Petushki*; 1969–1970). Nevertheless, his collected writings — including several imaginative essays, notes and marginalia, and a few unfinished works — do fill a slender volume. *Walpurgis Night, or the Steps of the Commander* (*Val'purgieva noch', ili shagi Komandora*) is the only complete play in Erofeev's oeuvre. It was intended, he said, to be the second and central play in a trilogy to be called *Three Nights*. Fragments of the first play in the trilogy, called *Dissidents, or Fanni Kaplan* (*Dissidenty, ili Fanni Kaplan*), are extant; the third play was never written. First published abroad in the émigré journal *Kontinent* in 1985, *Walpurgis Night* appeared for the first time in the Soviet Union in the April 1989 issue of *Teatr;* the play was subsequently published in several collections during the glasnost period. It is included in its entirety in the 1995 compendium of Erofeev's work, *Leave My Soul in Peace* (*Ostav'te moiu dushu v pokoe*). Staged at the Student Theater of Moscow State University, at the Theater on Malaia Bronnaia, and at several other theaters in Moscow and Saint Petersburg in the late 1980s and early 1990s, the play met mostly lukewarm reviews. *Walpurgis Night* was previously translated into English by Alexander Burry and Tatiana Tulchinsky (*Toronto Slavic Quarterly*, no. 9 [Summer 2004]: online); this volume is thus the second English translation of a complex and linguistically challenging work and the first print publication of the play in English.

Walpurgis Night has moments of humor and, perhaps more important, moments of transcendent faith in something beyond the dreariness and brutality of life in the late Soviet Union. These moments are rare, however, and the play is generally darker in tone than *Moscow to the End of the Line*. Whereas Venichka's death at the end of the *poema* is ambiguous (after all, Venichka wrote it after his murder), *Walpurgis Night* has a horrifyingly tragic end devoid of any hope of redemption. Insofar as Gurevich is an authorial character, Erofeev the playwright kills himself at the end of the fifth act. Comparing the literary suicides in *Moscow to the End of the Line* and *Walpurgis Night*, we could conclude that Erofeev had reached a point of exhaustion and perhaps despair by the time he wrote this play.

The plot of *Walpurgis Night* is rudimentary. Lev Isakovich Gurevich, an alcoholic member of the intelligentsia, is brought into a psychiatric hospital on the evening of April 30. He is involuntarily committed and installed in Ward 3. There he meets the other patients, a group of men with diverse delusions and obsessions, whose debates and monologues constitute the substance of the play. As they converse and proclaim, they are subjected to brutal psychiatric "treatments" at the hands of the nurses Tamarochka and Borenka "the Goon." By tricking Natalie, a kinder nurse and his former lover, Gurevich is able to obtain the keys to the medical supply cabinet and secure alcohol for a Walpurgis Night celebration. After all the patients have drunk the spirits, they fall ill and lose their sight; we realize that they have drunk methyl alcohol as one by one they die in agony. Gurevich, the last to die, is beaten ferociously in his last minutes by an enraged Borenka. The play closes with bodies strewn about the ward as the morning dawns.

More than thirty years after Erofeev's untimely death, this play will inevitably be read against the legend of the author. Even before Erofeev died of throat cancer in 1990, the legend had been created by his friends and his readers; in the years since, it has flourished. According to this legend, Erofeev managed to live freely as a liminal figure outside the boundaries of Soviet social and political convention. His drinking, his joblessness, and his peripatetic lifestyle all contributed to his being cast as a talented eccentric. It is ironic but not unusual in the context of twentieth-century Russian culture that the author, homeless and nearly destitute for much of his life, is now regarded as a genius of postmodern narrative. A sculpture has been installed on Ploshchad' Bor'by (the Square of Struggle) in Moscow, immortalizing Venichka's early-morning search for the hair of the dog at the opening of *Moscow to the End of the Line*. Reading the *poema* while riding the commuter train out to Petushki is a sort of pilgrimage made by Erofeev devotees. Erofeev's biography, though still rather murky, has been the subject of dozens of memoirs; it has nearly become hagiography, the writer cast as a martyr to the repressive Soviet state. The enduring fascination with Erofeev's life may derive from the need to believe that it was possible to live beyond the strictures of Soviet society. Like Vladimir Vysotsky, the celebrity bard poet of the Brezhnev era, Erofeev resisted the pressure to conform and to pursue conventional success. The relationship between Erofeev and society was symbiotic, however, insofar as Erofeev's peculiar genius seems to have required the absurdity of Soviet reality as the source of his satire and parody.

Walpurgis Night, like *Moscow to the End of the Line*, is soaked in alcohol on the levels of plot and narration. Here, too, drunkenness (or, more precisely, alcoholism) fuels the characters' speeches and motivates their actions. At times, Gurevich's rhetorical flights are inspired by inebriation, as are Venichka's. Venichka, however, strives toward the garden where the jasmine is always blooming and the nightingales never cease singing. He depends on alcohol for transcendence, for escape from quotidian Soviet life. Gurevich's quest, in contrast, is for oblivion, realized in blindness, the loss of his voice, and death. By the time Erofeev is writing *Walpurgis Night*, alcohol is no longer a magic potion or a liquor subject to transubstantiation: it is poison. In *Moscow to the End of the Line* love and alcohol are intricately interwoven in the image of the red-haired woman waiting in Petushki; in *Walpurgis Night* love—sullied at the outset by Gurevich's suspicion that Natalie has been unfaithful to him—is merely a pretense, a means of obtaining the keys to the supply cabinet. The absence of love (however fanciful) in the plot contributes significantly to the bleakness of the play.

It is curious that Erofeev turned to writing plays in the last years of his life, for he rarely attended the theater. On the evidence of this single play, it seems that the form allowed him to create pure verbal constructs, speeches linked or unlinked by logic (because the characters are madmen or alcoholics). The setting is minimal; the stage directions for the most part refer to characters' appearance or provide authorial commentary on the action. In some cases, Erofeev uses stage directions to give the reader (and presumably the director) insight into the emotions and thoughts of the characters. In respect to form, however, Erofeev is remarkably traditional. *Walpurgis Night* in the Russian version is subtitled "A Tragedy in Five Acts," and the play adheres closely to the classical structure of the tragedy. We have in the first act the exposition, with Gurevich's arrival and incarceration in the psychiatric hospital. The second act is the complication, with the mock trial of Rear Admiral Mikhalych and the cruel beatings of several patients at the hands of the medical staff. In the third act we have development of the action, as Gurevich symbolically seduces Natalie with his poetry and obtains the key to the supply cabinet. The culmination or catastrophe occurs in the fourth act when the patients drink the methyl alcohol Gurevich has stolen. The fifth act gives us the tragic denouement, as the inmates of Ward 3 die one by one, ending with Gurevich.

The setting of the play in a Soviet psychiatric hospital has both political and aesthetic significance. When Erofeev was writing, psychiatry in the Soviet Union was largely an instrument of state repression and punishment. Political dissidents were frequently confined to psychiatric hospitals in the 1970s; they were diagnosed with schizophrenia, subjected to brutal treatment, and forced to take mind-numbing drugs. The psychiatric hospital—or less euphemistically, the madhouse—functions as a microcosm of Soviet society. Ironically but entirely in keeping with the tradition of the trope in Russian literature, the patient-inmates are freer than those outside the walls of the hospital. Written off as madmen, they are free to express their ideas and opinions openly. Just as Aleksandr Solzhenitsyn populated his cancer ward with patients whose illnesses reflected the ways they had lived their lives, Erofeev creates a cast of characters who embody various ideologies. Prokhorov is a mouthpiece for Soviet jargon; his lines are largely propaganda slogans, and he has dictatorial tendencies. Seryozha Kleinmikhel is a utopian dreamer, unstained by the pragmatic cynicism of Soviet culture. Vova, an old man from the country, voices the neo-romanticism of Village Prose, a movement far from Erofeev's own literary inclinations. Stasik invents a fantastical garden with words, some of which he coins in his mad perorations. Gurevich stands at the center of this cacophony, a holy fool stubbornly insisting on the power of beauty. Indeed, he is a sort of encyclopedia of world culture; his lines are variously quotations from, references to, or catalogues of works of art, literature, and music.

A striking feature of this play is that Gurevich sometimes speaks in verse. His switching to verse seems spontaneous, a tic that he cannot control even when threatened with punishment. Though often banal and humorous, his "Shakespearean iambs" (as one of the doctor's assistants calls his unrhymed iambic pentameter) distinguish him from the other patients in the psychiatric ward and from the staff. Then the other patients take to speaking in verse, following Gurevich's example, and even stage a poetic performance at the beginning of the last act. Early in the play Gurevich tells the doctor that he is quite content in the Soviet Union except that he dislikes the "disrespect for the Word" that he senses around him. His identity as a poet puts him in an antagonistic relationship with the state, represented in *Walpurgis Night* by the staff of the psychiatric ward. Erofeev's adaptation of this Pushkinian theme resonates profoundly in the late Soviet period, for questions of accommodation, self-censorship, and coexistence with authority were highly relevant to the literary culture of those years.

Gurevich is half Jewish, which is obvious to other characters in the play and to Russian readers from his first name and his patronymic.

His Jewishness is significant for understanding the meaning of his life and death. Entrenched anti-Semitism was a given for Erofeev, an unalterable feature of Soviet culture. The other characters—especially Prokhorov, who speaks in official Soviet cant—casually cast anti-Semitic slurs and voice crude stereotypes. And while Gurevich resembles the author in many ways, his Jewishness is an additional, non-autobiographical feature that is clearly symbolic. It underscores his otherness and his status as a victim of irrational hatred.

Walpurgis Night is saturated with violence, both physical violence and violence done to the spirit. Erofeev's play is reminiscent in this respect of both Chekhov's short story "Ward No. 6" and Ken Kesey's 1962 book, *One Flew Over the Cuckoo's Nest*. Brutality is more graphic and more constant here than in *Moscow to the End of the Line*, making it a challenging work to experience. Borenka the Goon and Tamarochka embody cruelty toward the vulnerable and the weak. They enjoy administering various sadistic "treatments" to the patients and thus personify the immorality of Soviet power. Language is frequently an instrument of violence in the play as well. The speech of the hospital staff often consists of strings of profanities, ugly insults, and threats that accompany physical blows.

The title of the play is an amalgam of several cultural and literary references; the density of these within the title reflects Erofeev's use of quotation or echoing throughout the play. "Walpurgis Night" refers to the spring holiday marked traditionally by revelry, carousing, and excess. The holiday is best known to us through the Faust legend and the literary and musical works that developed it, most notably Goethe's *Faust*, Mendelssohn's oratorio, and Balanchine's ballet. Walpurgis Night ends at dawn on May 1. Thus the revelry in Erofeev's psychiatric ward takes on overtones of a witches' sabbath and ends with the dawn of May Day, in time for the Soviet celebration of Communist solidarity, with all of the patients lying dead. Walpurgis Night is exactly six months from All Souls' Day and is the pagan antipode to the ecclesiastical holiday. Erofeev, as we know, converted to Catholicism in 1987, near the end of his life. However, little in this play suggests faith or comfort in religious conviction;

Erofeev portrays the lives of his characters as hellish and their deaths as pointless.

The second part of the play's title, *The Steps of the Commander*, refers to the Don Juan legend and its literary manifestations. The most direct reference is to Aleksandr Blok's 1912 poem "The Steps of the Commander" ("Shagi komandora") from his *Retribution* cycle. Inevitably, the subtitle calls to mind Aleksandr Pushkin's play "The Stone Guest" ("Kammenyi gost'"), which is also based on the Don Juan legend and is a source for Blok's poem. As in these two seminal reference texts, the steps of the commander in Erofeev's play suggest impending destiny. The approaching steps are retributive, promising punishment for betrayal. In Pushkin's play, Don Juan has whimsically seduced Doña Anna and taunted fate; Blok's poetic persona has betrayed the ideal of the Beautiful Lady and squandered his talent. One suspects that both variants inform Erofeev's Gurevich, for he manipulates others—first and foremost Natalie, but the other patients as well—for his own purposes. And he has abused his poetic talent, veering from the sublime to the vulgar in his verses, unoriginally patching together lines from myriad sources.

Walpurgis Night is densely packed with cultural, literary, and historical references beyond the Faust and Don Juan legends. In fact, the play includes even more concentrated clusters of allusions than does *Moscow to the End of the Line*. Erofeev's references are often thematically significant; place-names, literary echoes, and musical motifs enhance or contrast parodically with the characters or plot of the play. In other cases, these references seem intended to create sound patterns, sonic associations quite free of connotative connection. Gurevich transforms Francisco Goya to General Franco and Gaius Julius Caesar to César Cui to Tsezar Solodar, weaving a cultural pastiche. It remains for Erofeev scholars to tease out the significance of the many references included in *Walpurgis Night*, as they have done for *Moscow to the End of the Line*. Some references will be best appreciated aurally, however, as Erofeev follows Marina Tsvetaeva in privileging sound over sense in poetically linking images.

The levels of language used by the characters in the play vary widely, although this contrast is felt more strongly in the original Russian than in English translation. Bureaucratic jargon jostles with colloquialisms, poetic flights are interrupted by profane interjections. Linguistic mélange—a striking aspect of *Moscow to the End of the Line*—is a structural feature of this play, for most of the characters are associated with a level or type of language. The stylistic complexity of *Walpurgis Night* presents a challenge to the translator. The many puns and idioms that Erofeev embeds in the text also pose difficulties for translation. Marian Schwartz's translation renders both the sense and the spirit of the play. The English-language reader experiences the temporary escape that poetic language offers the patients in the psychiatric ward (or the Soviet Union). The brutality that pervades the world of the hospital is conveyed in equally ugly English profanity. And Gurevich's senseless roaring (*ryk*) at the end of the play is a tragic descent into voicelessness that signifies the destruction of poetry in all languages.

Karen Ryan

Walpurgis Night,
or the Steps of
the Commander

CAST

ADMITTING DOCTOR at the psych hospital

HIS TWO FEMALE ASSISTANTS. One, skinny and frail, wears glasses. More of a secretary than an assistant. The other, Zinaida Nikolaevna, crimson and immense.

HEAD PHYSICIAN IGOR LVOVICH RANINSON

PROKHOROV, monitor on Ward 3 and dictator on 2

GUREVICH

ALYOKHA, aka the Dissident, Prokhorov's sword-bearer

VOVA, a melancholy old guy from the countryside

SERYOZHA KLEINMIKHEL, a milquetoast, a daydreamer

VITYA

STASIK, declaimer and floriculturalist

KOLYA

PASHKA ERYOMIN, Ward 3's Young Communist League organizer, or Komsorg

REAR ADMIRAL MIKHALYCH

NURSE LUCY

NURSE NATALIE

NURSE AIDE TAMAROCHKA

MALE NURSE BORENKA, BORIS ANATOLIEVICH, aka the Goon

3

KHOKHULYA, sexual mystic and Satanist

FAT TECHS who carry the dead bodies out on stretchers in the
    last act

        All the action takes place through the night of April 30
                and into the wee hours of May Day.

ACT ONE

Also the prologue. The admitting office. To the audience's left, the jury: The senior admitting physician looks like the composer Georgy Sviridov, with a nearly square kisser and perfectly square glasses. To either side of him, two ladies in white coats: Zinaida Nikolaevna, who takes up nearly half the proscenium, and Valentina, spacey, bespectacled, hunched over her papers. Behind them, Borenka, also known as the Goon, a male nurse, paces up and down, but more about him ahead. Across the table, L. I. Gurevich, who has just been brought in by meat wagon (ambulance).

DOCTOR:	Your name, patient?
GUREVICH:	Gurevich.
DOCTOR:	So, Gurevich. How can you confirm you're Gurevich and not . . . Do you have any papers on you?
GUREVICH:	No papers. I don't like them. René Descartes once said that—
DOCTOR:	(*straightening his glasses*) Name and patronymic?
GUREVICH:	Whose? Descartes'?

DOCTOR:	No, no, patient. Your name and patronymic!
GUREVICH:	Lev Isakovich.
DOCTOR:	(*under his glasses, to the bespectacled Valentina*) Make a note of that.
VALENTINA:	Sorry. A note of what?
DOCTOR:	Everything! A note of everything! Are your parents living? Why should you lie, Gurevich? Unless you aren't Gurevich at all. So, I repeat, are your parents living?
GUREVICH:	Both are living and both their names are —
DOCTOR:	I'm curious to know their names.
GUREVICH:	Isaak Gurevich. And my mama is Rozalia Pavlovna.
DOCTOR:	Also Gurevich?
GUREVICH:	Yes. But she's Russian.
DOCTOR:	Well, and what is your relationship with your mother?
GUREVICH:	You are tactless, doctor. What is "What is your relationship with your mother?" supposed to mean? What is your relationship with yours, assuming you're not an orphan?
DOCTOR:	Notice, patient, I'm holding my temper. I would ask the same of you. And who do you love more, your mama or your

papa? Medically speaking, this is not at all irrelevant.

GUREVICH: My papa, I guess. When he and I swam the Hellespont—

DOCTOR: (*to bespectacled Valentina*) Make a note there. Loves his papa the Jew more than his Russian mama. But what took you to the Hellespont? Unless my knowledge of geography fails me, that is not our territory.

GUREVICH: Well, that depends. All territory is ours. Or rather, it will be. They just don't let us go there—something to do with peace-making, apparently. So we've made do with one-sixth of the inhabitable dry land.

DOCTOR: So, is it very wide, this Hellespont?

GUREVICH: A few Bosporuses.

DOCTOR: You mean you measure distance in Bos-poruses? You're in luck, patient. Your ward mate is a man who measures time in nightstands and stools. Birds of a feather. So what's a Bosporus?

GUREVICH: That's so easy even you can understand. When I leave the house in the morn-ing for hooch, my trip to the store takes exactly 670 of my steps, and according to Brockhaus, that's the exact width of the Bosporus.

DOCTOR: So far so good. Do you take that walk very often?

GUREVICH:	That depends. Not as often as others. Unlike them, though, I do it without making a big effin' deal of it. Me—just when I'm sad.
DOCTOR:	Let's leave your sadness out of this. The question is where you get the money. Did you cross that Bosporus of yours every day? This is very important.
GUREVICH:	You know, I don't care what the job is. I'm willing to do anything—a mass sowing of buckwheat and millet. Or vice versa. Right now I've got a job at a hardware store. I'm their Tatar.
ZINAIDA NIKOLAEVNA:	How much do they pee you?
GUREVICH:	They pay me exactly what my Homeland thinks right and proper. If that seemed like too little, and I got to sulking, say, the Homeland would track me down and ask, "Lev, this isn't enough for you? Maybe we should give you a little more." And I'd say, "I'm fine, Homeland, back off. You don't have jackshit either."
DOCTOR:	(*feeling superior*) I see you're a freewheeling sailor, not a hardware store Tatar. Stand up. Feet together. Close your eyes. Arms forward.

Gurevich does what he's told.

GUREVICH:	May I sit down?
DOCTOR:	Yes, yes. That will do. We're clear on everything, essentially. There's just one

	more detail. I'm not asking whether you're married or not, but <u>do you have a woman dear to your heart, someone to share your life's journey?</u>
GUREVICH:	Of course I do. I mean, of course I did. When she and I were swimming across the Hindu Kush, she smashed her beautiful head on the reefs of British Samoa. At that moment (*Gurevich is on the verge of tears*), at that very moment—fate knocked the baton from the maestro's hands. I drowned but washed up. Are you happy I did?
DOCTOR:	From the Hindu Kush?
GUREVICH:	Yes. What's washing up from the Hindu Kush for someone who's conquered the Dardanelles?
DOCTOR:	Oh ho! It's rare that we get a patient like this. I'm glad you didn't drown. But when you were swimming, did you take a bottle along?
GUREVICH:	And how! A real armor-piercer! Ammonium acetate. Sharks can't stand it. The minute a shark turns up, you pour a little ammonium acetate on your head and your girlfriend's, and that's it. The sharks won't back down, and eventually they lose their empty heads. Well, they did lick my girlfriend's calves in parting, but being jealous would have been ridiculous in that situation. Now when it came to Karakorum . . .

DOCTOR:	What is today's date? The year? The month?
GUREVICH:	What's the difference? Days, millennia — that's all so trivial for Russia.
DOCTOR:	I see. Tell me, patient, have you ever experienced any delusions or illusions, chimeras or otherworldly voices?
GUREVICH:	You know, I can't give you that pleasure. It's never happened. But . . .
DOCTOR:	So there is a "but" after all?
GUREVICH:	Yes, about those chimeras. Why on earth, for instance, did I travel the world over, cross the Kunlun, climb to the top of Kon-Tiki—and the only thing I learned from it all was that the best place in Arkhangelsk to turn in your empty wine bottles is on Rosa Luxembourg Street!
DOCTOR:	Anything else peculiar?
GUREVICH:	Lots. Say you decide you want nothing but Boötes the Plowman in the sky. No other constellations. And that under this Boötes, something gets taken away from me, something substantial but not the most precious.

The doctor and nurses are getting nervous. Behind their backs, Borenka the Goon is pacing back and forth serenely.

(*continues*) But all thoughts of Boötes and the Pleiades flew from my mind when I started noticing something peculiar about myself. I discovered that when I picked up my left foot, I couldn't pick up my right simultaneously. I found that distressing. I shared my bewilderment with Prince Golitsyn.

I guess one would have to jump

The doctor signals with his left eye for Valentina to write this down. She bows her pockmarked head lazily.

So he and I were drinking and drinking and drinking to bring clarity to our thoughts. And I asked him in a whisper—not wanting to disturb anyone—not that there was anyone to disturb, we were alone, no one there but us. Anyway, see, so I wouldn't disturb anyone, I whispered, "Why is our clock going backward?" He looked hard at me and then at the clock and said, "Yes, one can hardly tell; yes, you seem to have been drinking a little, but it's only my clock going backward."

DOCTOR: Drinking is bad for your health, Lev Isakovich.

GUREVICH: As if I didn't know. Telling me that now is like telling the Moor of Venice, say, who has just been shaken by his deed—like telling him that crushing a windpipe and trachea can lead to paralysis of the expiratory center as a result of asphyxiation.

DOCTOR: That's quite enough, I think. So, you and Prince Golitsyn. And have you had occasion to sip vodka with any viscounts, counts, or marquises?

GUREVICH:	Have I ever. For instance, Count Tolstoy calls me up—
DOCTOR:	Lev?
GUREVICH:	Why Lev necessarily? If it's a count, then it's got to be Lev? I'm Lev, too, but I'm no count. My grandson Lev calls me up and says he has two bottles of ginger vodka on the table but nothing for snacks besides two jokes about Chapaev—
DOCTOR:	And does this Count Tolstoy live very far away?
GUREVICH:	On the contrary. The Novokuznetskaya metro station, and not far from there at all. If you haven't drunk ginger vodka in a while . . .
DOCTOR:	And what about Joseph de Maistre? Viscount de Bragelonne? You could invite them through the back door and glug straight from the bottle, that—what do you call it?—hooch.
GUREVICH:	Gladly. Though there'd better be some spindle trees by the door. Anemones aren't a bad idea either. But there are rumors going around, you know, that they've all emigrated.
DOCTOR:	The anemones?
GUREVICH:	If only the anemones. But you know it's the Bragelonnes, the Josephs, and the crocuses, too. Every one of them running away. But why? And where? Take me,

for example, I like it here very much. If there's something I don't like, it's the ban on the nomadic life. And the disrespect for the Word. As for all the rest . . .

DOCTOR: (*his authoritative tone becomes exaggerated*) Well, but what if disaster befalls our Homeland? After all, it's no secret that our enemies live solely for the thought of destabilizing us, and decisively. . . . Do you understand me? You and I are not speaking of trifles. (*Addressing Zinaida Nikolaevna.*) How many ethnicities, languages, tribes do we have in Russia?

ZINAIDA NIKOLAEVNA: Damned if I know. Must be five hundred.

DOCTOR: There, you see? Five hundred. And what do you think, patient, in the event of certain circumstances—in the face of our opponent—which tribe would be the most trustworthy? You're an educated man, you know a thing or two about spindle trees and anemones—and you know there's a reason they're running away from us. And here we have a storm breaking out. Whose service are you in, Lev Isakovich?

GUREVICH: I'm opposed to all wars in general. War *pacifist* decimates soldiers, destroys ranks, and stains uniforms. Grand Duke Konstantin Pavlovich. But that doesn't mean anything. If ever my Native Land finds itself on the brink of disaster . . .

DOCTOR: (*in Valentina's direction*) Write that
                                down, too.

GUREVICH: If ever my Native Land finds itself on the
                                brink of catastrophe, if ever my Native
                                Land says, "Lev! Quit drinking, get up,
                                and come out of oblivion," then . . .

*The room comes to life. A clatter of heels coming from the right—
and Nurse Natalie sails into the admitting room swiftly but without fuss. Her eyes take up nearly half of her smiling physiognomy.
A dimple in her cheek. Hair at the nape, solid black, fastened by an
amazing pin. She exudes Slavic tranquillity and meekness—but
Andalusia as well.*

DOCTOR: You've come at a good time, Natalia
                                Alexeyevna.

*The usual exchange of greetings among the ladies, and so forth.
Natalie takes a seat next to Zinaida.*

NATALIE: A newcomer. . . . Gurevich? It's been
                                ages.

DOCTOR: We're essentially concluding our inter-
                                view with the patient. No distractions,
                                Natalia Alexeyevna, and no side deals. All
                                that remains is to clarify a few facts—and
                                then off to the ward.

GUREVICH: (*livened up by Natalie's presence, con-
                                tinues*) We were speaking about our
                                Native Land and disaster. And so, I love
                                Russia. It occupies one-sixth of my soul.
                                Probably a little more now.

Laughter in the room.

> Every ordinary citizen should be a brave
> warrior, just as all regular urine should be
> a bright amber color. (*Quoting Kheraskov*
> *inspiredly.*)

     Yet poised our country to defend,
     The universe we gladly battle.

There's just one consideration holding
me back. I, a morally despicable whiner,
am simply unworthy of fighting for such
a Homeland.

DOCTOR:
And why is that? We're going to cure you
here and—

GUREVICH:
And just what is it you're going to cure?
There's still not a chance in hell I'll
figure out what kind of tank it is or where
it's going. Naturally, I'm ready to throw
myself under any tank, with or without a
string of grenades.

ZINAIDA NIKOLAEVNA:
Why without?

GUREVICH:
The foe goes flying even if men throw
themselves under without anything. My
advice to you is: read more. You know, if
there isn't a single tank anywhere nearby,
I'm sure to find an embrasure. It doesn't
matter whose. I'll fall on it posthaste,
chest first—and lie on it, lie there until
our Red banner rises over the Capitol.

DOCTOR:
That's enough clowning around, I think.
As you yourself will discover before the
day is out, we have more than our share
of jesters here. How do you assess your

	overall condition? Do you seriously believe your brain is undamaged?
GUREVICH:	(*while the pain-in-the-neck doctor cinematographically and deductively taps his fingers on the table*) What about yours?
DOCTOR:	(*biliously*) I asked you to only answer my questions, patient. I'll answer yours when you're fully cured. So what about your overall condition, in your opinion?
GUREVICH:	That's hard for me to say. Such a strange feeling. Involved-in-nothing-ness. Excited-by-nothing-ness. Inclined-toward-no-one-ness. It's like being engaged to someone, but who, when, or why is beyond your ken. It's like being occupied, and occupied for a reason, under a mutual assistance and friendship pact, but occupied nonetheless. There's an apparently-involved-in-nothing-ness, but also a not-crucified-on-anything-ness, a not-vomiting-over-anything-ness. Simply, you sense a grace inside you— but that's not quite right. Oh, like being in your stepmother's womb.

his description of madness - is he aware?

Applause.

DOCTOR:	You think you're not being clear, patient. You're mistaken. We'll knock the funny business out of you. I hope that for all your tendency toward cynicism and big talk, you show respect for our medicine and don't go making trouble on the wards.

GUREVICH: (*with a quick glance at Natalie straight-
                    ening her white coat*)

                    My papa used to tell me, "Lev, my
                        boy,
                    You'll be a bon vivant when you
                        grow up!"
                    No such luck. Ever since I was a
                        teen,
                    I've been learning to obey
                    Everyone—assuming they deserve
                        it. I've
                    Worn a straitjacket since I was born.
                    But when it comes to—

                    iambs

DOCTOR: (*frowning, interrupts him*) I believe I've
                    already asked you more than once not to
                    clown around. You're in admitting, not
                    on stage. You could speak like a human
                    being without those . . . those . . .

ZINAIDA NIKOLAEVNA: (*prompts him*) Shakespearean iambs.

DOCTOR: That's it, iambs. We've got enough hassle
                    without that.

GUREVICH: Fine. I'll stop. You were talking about our
                    medicine and whether I respect it. Re-
                    spect is too mundane a word, truth be
                    told, and flat-footed.

                    But I—I love her—no buffoonery,
                    No funny faces, no sticking out my
                        tongue.
                    I love her every rise and fall,
                    Her every try at doctoring ills,
                    Her infirmities of body and soul,
                    Her primacy within the Universe,

ode to medicine?

Her mind that doesn't fade, and —
thus — I love
Her eyes, her tail, her mane, her
mouth, her . . .

*Throughout this tirade, Borenka the Goon has been creeping up
on the declaimer from behind, waiting for the signal to grab him by
the scruff of his neck and drag him off.*

DOCTOR:
Well, well, well. That will do, patient.
A madhouse is no place to show off how
smart you are. Can you tell me exactly
when you were brought here the last
time?

GUREVICH:
Of course. Only — you see? — I measure
time a little differently. Naturally, not by
Fahrenheit, or nightstands, or Réaumurs.
But a tad differently. For instance, I care
about the distance between this day and
the autumnal equinox or, oh, the sum-
mer solstice, or some other dirty trick.
Wind direction, for instance. We — the
majority — you see, we don't even know,
if the wind's northeasterly, which way it's
actually blowing: *from* or *to* the northeast.
We just don't give a damn. But Agamemnon, king of Mycenae, he put his favorite,
his youngest daughter, Iphigenia, under
the sacrificial knife just so the wind would
be southwest rather than otherwise.

DOCTOR:
(*noticing the patient's agitation, gives
everyone else the signal*) Yes, but you're
avoiding my question. You've been
carried off by a nor'easter.

Everyone laughs except Natalie.

	So when was the last time you were brought here?
GUREVICH:	I don't remember. I don't remember exactly. Even the winds. I only remember it was the day the Kuwaiti sheikh Abdallah al-Salem al-Sabah approved a new government led by hereditary prince Sabah al-Salim al-Sabah eighty-four days from the summer solstice. Yes, yes, to be quite precise, that day an event occurred that etched itself in the memory of millions for five whole years. The same empty wine bottle that had cost 12 or 17 kopeks, depending on volume, that day, well, they all cost 20.
DOCTOR:	*(curbing the ladies' giggling with a look)* So you believe that no more significant event in the history of Soviet Russia has occurred in the past five years?
GUREVICH:	Not at all. Sure . . . I don't remember. No.
DOCTOR:	It looks like your memory is starting to betray you—and not just your memory. The last time your diagnosis was acute alcoholic intoxication bordering on polyneuritis. Now the situation is going to be more complicated. You'll have to stay here a good six months.
GUREVICH:	*(jumps up, and so does everyone else)* Six months?

Borenka lowers Gurevich to his chair with trained hands.

DOCTOR: Why so surprised, patient? You present a
                 wonderful syndrome. I'll tell you a secret.
                 Recently we've begun hospitalizing even
                 those who, to the casual eye, don't exhibit
                 a single symptom of psychological dis-
                 turbance. But we must not forget about
                 these patients' capacity for involuntary
                 or intentional dissimulation. As a rule,
                 these people don't commit a single anti-
                 social deed, a single criminal act, don't
                 show even the slightest hint of nervous
                 imbalance, to the end of their days. But
                 this is exactly why they are dangerous and
                 must be subjected to treatment. If only
                 because of their private disinclination to
                 adapt socially.

GUREVICH: *(in ecstasy)* That's great!

                 No, it's true, I do revere the march
                 Of medicine, its progress and
                      triumphs.
                 Its many glories—a spit in the eye,
                 Amazing all the continents.
                 I love its smugness, its audacity,
                      And its tail, again, its . . .

DOCTOR: *(his distinguished voice shifts to a lordly
                 tone)* I thought you and I had come to
                 an agreement long ago about these . . .
                 these iambs, patient. I've been around,
                 and I promise you that this will roll off
                 you after the very first week of our proce-
                 dures. Along with all your sarcasm. In a

	couple of weeks you'll be saying normal things like a normal human being. Are you a bit of a poet?
GUREVICH:	You mean they cure you of that, too?
DOCTOR:	Why would you say that? Who do you write like? Who's your favorite?
GUREVICH:	Martynov, naturally.
ZINAIDA NIKOLAEVNA:	Leonid Martynov?
GUREVICH:	Of course not. Nikolai Martynov. And George Dantes.
NATALIE:	(*taking advantage of the general excitement*) So, Lev, now you're scratching like Dantes?
GUREVICH:	Oh, no, I did write in my own style before, but that tapped out. A month ago I was scribbling a good ten poems a day. As a rule, about nine of them were unforgettable, five or six epoch-making, and two or three immortal. Now I'm not. Now I've decided to improvise in the style of Nikolai Nekrasov. Want one about socialist competition?
DOCTOR:	Well, why not? Socialist competition is, after all— *oxymoron*
GUREVICH:	I'll be very brief. Seven guys get together and argue over how many eggs they can squeeze out of each laying hen. The district center people and the roosters have no suspicion of this, naturally. All around

are sows, pennants, a verdurous mass in
the silos—and here the men are arguing:

> A hundred seventy, said Roman.
> A hundred eighty, said Demian.
> Five hundred, said Luka.
> Two thousand one hundred seventy,
> Said the Gubin brothers,
> Ivan and Mitrodor.
> Old Man Pakhom thought long and
>   hard
> And spoke, an eye cast to the
>   ground:
> One hundred thirty-one thousand
>   four hundred fourteen.
> And then Prov said, A mil.

Shall I go on?

DOCTOR: *(gesturing no)* No, no, no need. Boris
Anatolievich, Natalia Alexeyevna, be so
kind as to escort the patient to Ward 4.
And immediately to the bathroom. *(To
Gurevich.)* I trust that matters have not
reached the point of hydrophobia for
you, have they?

GUREVICH: Not that I've noticed. If you don't count
the untold number of bloody associations
I have with the bath. There's that Myce-
naean king Agamemnon I was mentioning. When he got back from Pergamum,
he was hacked to death in the bath. And
Marat, the great mouthpiece of the
revolu—

ZINAIDA NIKOLAEVNA: *(ignoring him and addressing the doctor)*

Why 4? There's nothing but smelly piddlers there. He'll waste away there and start having suicidal thoughts. I think he'd be better off in 3. Prokhorov's there, and Eryomin. They'll crack down on him there.

DOCTOR: "Suicidal thoughts," you say. (*To Gurevich*.) One last question for you. Have you ever, if only in deepest, darkest secret, had thoughts of doing away with yourself or anyone close to you? Because 4 isn't 3, and occasionally we have to keep our eyes peeled.

GUREVICH: Hand on heart, I've already dispatched one person. I was . . . I don't remember how old I was at the time, not very, but it all happened three days before the new moon. More than anything else then, I felt the hostility of my bald uncle, an admirer of Lazar Kaganovich, bawdy jokes, and chicken soup. My towhead friend Edik brought me the poison, and he said the poison was foolproof and fast-acting. I poured it all into my uncle's chicken soup, and—wouldn't you know it?— exactly twenty-six years later he expired in terrible agony.

DOCTOR: Mmm hmm. The hell with your uncle. What about you? Have you ever been tempted to lay hands on yourself?

GUREVICH: There have been times. Just the day before yesterday even, during the Flood.

DOCTOR: The worldwide flood?

GUREVICH: Definitely not worldwide. It all started
with the driving rains in Orekhovo-
Zuevo. Lately in Russia we've started
having runs of bizarre local disasters:
outside Kostroma, in broad daylight,
nursing infants, bulldozers, and all that
sort of thing rocketed up to the heavens.
And no one's surprised by these shenani-
gans. More or less the same happened in
Orekhovo-Zuevo. The rains lashed down
for seven days and seven nights, without
letup or mercy; the earthly earth disappeared along with the heavenly heavens.

DOCTOR: What the hell took you—a Tatar from a
Moscow hardware store—to Orekhovo-
Zuevo?

GUREVICH: How sad to be a Tatar—to the grave!
Moonlighting a little in the boonies:
As conformist and nonconformist
     both,
And usurper. An anthropophagite
Assigned the role of Japanese spy
At the Institute of Permafrost. . . .

In short, when the elements came crashing down on the city, I had a dugout
and twelve valiant aboriginal rowers.
There was no one and nothing else on
the waves. And then—I don't remember how many days we'd been floating or
how many nights before the solstice—
the water began subsiding, and the spire

of the Young Communist City Committee building poked out of the water. We
moored. But afterward—what a spectacle: the devastation of hearts, the howls
inside the destroyed buildings. I decided
to kill myself by throwing myself onto the
City Committee spire.

*The doctor, holding his head, makes it clear to Boris and Natalie
that they should take the patient to the ward immediately.*

One more second, fellas! When my
throat was over the spike and the spike
was under my throat, one rower friend of
mine, to amuse me and distract me from
my spiritual gloom, posed this riddle:
"Two piglets run eight versts in an hour.
How many piglets will run one verst in
an hour?" It was at this point that I realized I was losing my mind. And here I
am. With you.

wtf.

*Half rises from his chair, helped with exaggerated courtesy by the
Goon.*

Ever since that day, my head's been a
jumble. *Nacht und Nebel.* Everything's
mixed up: the calves, the piglets, Mamai
Hill, Malakhov Hill.

NATALIE: Is your head spinning, Lev? Go quietly,
                        quietly.

Natalie leads him by his left arm, Borenka his right.

It will all be over soon, they'll put you to
bed.

GUREVICH:	(*goes quietly*) For some reason, though, everything's confused, mixed up, the piglets, the hills, Henry Ford and Ernest Rutherford, Rembrandt and Willy Brandt.
DOCTOR:	(*following him*) Ward 3. Glucose, piracetam.
GUREVICH:	(*moves off with his escorts, his voice becoming increasingly muffled*) Upton Sinclair and Sinclair Lewis. Sinclair Lewis and Lewis Carroll. Vera Maretskaya and Maya Plisetskaya. Jacques Offenbach and Ludwig Feuerbach. (*Now barely audibly.*) Viktor Bokov and Vladimir Nabokov. Enrico Caruso and Robinson Crusoe.

Curtain.

ACT TWO

Before the curtain rises, five minutes of bad, ponderous music. When the curtain does rise, the audience sees Ward 3, with barred windows and an archway to the adjoining Ward 2. To prevent inter-ward diffusion, the exchange of information, and so on, the archway is filled with a cot, on which lies Vitya, with his huge belly, which he can't stop stroking. Licking his lips at something, he wears a smile both horrifying and bashful. An inspired Stasik dashes around the ward strictly on the diagonal, his neck bent down to the left and up to the right. Occasionally he declaims something, occasionally he freezes in an unexpected pose — giving a Pioneer salute, for ex-ample — and then the declamations cease. But no one knows for how long.

Seryozha Kleinmikhel, still quite young, is sitting on his cot almost perfectly still, occasionally climbing down, constantly clutch-ing his heart. He's covered in hair and lichens, with an odd curl to his lips. On the next cot Kolya and meek old Vova, both silent so far, are holding hands. From time to time, Kolya drools and Vova wipes his mouth. Still lying down, his head covered by a sheet, in antici-pation of a tribunal, is Pashka Eryomin, the ward's Young Commu-nist League organizer, which is to say, their Komsorg. On the cot to the right is Khokhulya, who hasn't raised his eyelids; a sexual mystic and Satanist. But the main attraction, of course, is in the center: the autocratic and pimply Prokhorov, Ward 3's indefatigable monitor,

and his sword-bearer, Alyokha, known as the Dissident, who are con-
ducting (or rather, concluding) a trial in the case of Rear Admiral
Mikhalych.

PROKHOROV: If you were merely a snake, Mikhalych, that would be all right. A snake's a snake. But you're no black mamba. There's a South African snake called that, the black mamba. Its bite snuffs you out thirty seconds before it strikes! To the center, you son of a bitch!

His fat sword-bearer, Alyokha, ties the rear admiral's arms behind his back with a towel. Thrown to his knees, the rear admiral has lost all hope of any quarter.

                       You scum! How were you so lucky as to rise to the unprecedented rank of KGB rear admiral? I think you're really a KGB bosun and not a rear admiral at all!

ALYOKHA: Midshipman, he's a midshipman. I can tell from his ugly mug, he's a midshipman!

PROKHOROV: So now, midshipman, Alyokha here and I have totted up all your deeds. One would have been plenty. On September 1 of this past year you were sitting behind the wheel of a South Korean liner, right? The result is there for all to see: Chersonese and Coventry in ruins. I'm only amazed at the sophistication of the action. In all his attacks, the only victims were old men, women, and children! All the rest . . . all the rest—it was as if that hammer hadn't flown by them! So now,

	bosun, the gray hair of all these old men is clamoring for you, the tears of all the orphans, the guts of all the widows — they're clamoring for you! Alyokha!
ALYOKHA:	Yes, here I am.
PROKHOROV:	Tell me and all the Russian people: When was this murderer caught red-handed for selling our Kurils at the Preobrazhensky market?
ALYOKHA:	The day before yesterday.
MIKHALYCH:	(*bellows*) It's all a lie. The day before yesterday I was here, I didn't leave the ward or go anywhere — you're all witnesses — and Nurse Lucy fed me millet with gravy.
PROKHOROV:	That doesn't mean anything. You shithead. The day before, you managed to conduct electronic espionage over the Arctic Ocean basin without leaving the ward. The materials from the preliminary investigation don't lie. Judge for yourself, you little bastard: If you weren't an admiral, could you have made up the 107 pages of material for the preliminary investigation?
MIKHALYCH:	Ne-never.
PROKHOROV:	So here we are in the experts club: What? Where? Why? Why the Kurils now? Iturup for a bottle of Andropovka, and on credit at that? Kunashir for practically nothing. And maybe these political

operators, maybe those cuntfaces, just set
you up for all this?

Mikhalych tries in vain to bellow something in his own defense.

Not only that, this bosun was going to
bargain away to the CIA a map of the
Soviet Union's points of beverage pur-
chase. And while he was at it, dismem-
ber our blue-eyed sister Belarus and farm
her out to Misha Sokolov, dictator of
Cameroon.

STASIK: (*sauntering by, as usual*) Yes. Things
like that don't get you a pat on the head.
I propose removing his trousers and
firing mortars—

PROKHOROV: Stop. I'm not finished. This cur of a midshipman had this other intention as well,
since he had nothing to sell—in one
week he managed to drink up the mind,
honor, and conscience of our era. He
intended to sell off overseas the last two
national pearls we had: our ballet and
our subway. The deal was all set when this
double-dealer of ours made a little mis-
take about his clients from Manhattan.
When he went down into the subway
with one of them to put in the right fare,
the stupid Yankee businessman decided
he was looking at the ballet. And when
he took him to the ballet . . .

General rumble of condemnation.

Grisha! Komsorg! Throw off your sheet.

	Don't be afraid. You're not being tried today. Speak your piece, comrade!
PASHKA ERYOMIN:	(*who responds only when they call him Grisha*) Well, it's very simple. Why should our State treat this boa constrictor for free? He should be killed hanging upside down!
KOLYA:	Yes, that's what Oriental despots used to do with all Mussulmen. They threw their heads back and poured in a glug of melted lead. Or cold vermouth.
STASIK:	Better to shoot him with a crossbow.
KOLYA:	A crossbow from two and a half fields away.
STASIK:	Where are we supposed to get a crossbow? We might cobble a mortar together out of something. We could get laundry soap and a few aiguillettes from the nurse.
ALYOKHA:	Hah! Why don't you ask her for some galloons, too? I think we should hand this monster over to Vitenka to eat!

Shouts of approval. Everyone turns toward Vitya. But Vitya, who hasn't stopped smiling and stroking his belly, shakes his pink head in a sign of refusal.

| PROKHOROV: | Pray, Mikhalych! Pray for the last time, admiral! |
| MIKHALYCH: | (*dropping his head as far as it will go, mutters something very quickly, approxi-* |

	mately the following) Dying for Mother Moscow, our capital supreme, is nothing to dread; spend some time in the Kremlin, it's good for your head; if you learn what Lenin has to teach, you'll extend your mind's and hands' reach; the Soviet Union's the whole world's beacon; Moscow, where beauty flows, stirs cold dread in our foes.
PROKHOROV:	Yes, yes, yes, yes.
MIKHALYCH:	(*quaking, continues, and just as irrelevantly as before*) If in Moscow you've never been, then pure beauty you've never seen; with the Communists ahead of you, you'll always know the thing to do; a Soviet patriot always acts like a zealot; a tempered ideology brings soldiers courage, energy.
PROKHOROV:	Enough, midshipman! A brilliant prayer book. I don't think we need any crossbows. Just dissolve him in some chemical reagent so all that's left of him by evening is protoplasm. Only, why do we need any extra protoplasm in our department? You can hardly breathe because of it as is. Put him before the tribunal! Kolya, wipe off your drool. What do you think, Kolya—is there a lot of protoplasm in our department?
KOLYA:	A whole lot. I can't anymore.
PROKHOROV:	That's obvious. A tribunal. Of course, right now he's pathetic, this anti-party

leader, this anti-state figure, this anti-popular hero, veteran of three counter-revolutions: he's a helpless orphan. Obviously, you wouldn't last long on modest FBI assignments. All his mutterings and prayers—that's the usual posturing of our longtime foes. It's the longtime posturing of our usual foes. It's the hostile eternity of our poseurs.

Prokhorov paces enthusiastically.

It's these anti-Kremlin dreamers who are counting on our leniency. But we live in very harsh times, when you're better off using words like "leniency" as little as possible. It's only in wartime that you can joke with death, whereas in peacetime people don't. A tribunal. In the name of the people, bosun Mikhalych, a vigorous maniac in a Budyonny helmet and guard dog of the Pentagon, is sentenced to hanging for life. And to probationary imprisonment in all the fortresses of Russia—at one go!

Almost universal applause.

But for now, for want of supplies, bind him tighter to the bed. Let him think over his last words.

Alyokha and Pashka dump the admiral into bed and bind him—with sheets and towels—so that he can't budge a single one of his limbs or his member.

Lucy bursts onto the ward, drawn by the executioners' groans and the victim's deafening growls.

LUCY: What's going on here, boys? Leave him
                               alone. A day doesn't pass without you
                               taking the law into your hands. Where's
                               the extra cot?

Opens the cupboard and takes out a set of clean linen and ener-
getically flings it over the flat mattress.

                               Rounds soon. Be quiet!

Alyokha quietly takes meek Lucy by the shoulders, thrusting out
his belly and his furuncle eyes simultaneously, makes languorous
dance moves around her, and then sings his crowning glory, first
slapping himself on the belly and giving his head a shake.

ALYOKHA: I look forward in my dreams
                               To my hospital, to the screams,
                               And, still longer in my dreams,
                               To the way your booty gleams.

PROKHOROV: Alyokha! The chorus!

ALYOKHA: Alyokha's smokin' on his guitar,
                               I've gotta make that redhead mine!
                               Alyokha's smokin' on his guitar,
                               I've gotta make that redhead mine!
                               Poom! Poom! Poom! Poom!

Slapping his belly.

                               I've gotta,
                               I've gotta,
                               I've gotta make that redhead mine!
                               Poom! Poom! Poom! Poom!
                               She's unhooked all her hooks
                               And flung her clothes wide open.
                               The breath of life has
                               Barely left her nostrils.

The midshipman's pissed himself.
The bosun's gnawing at the deck!
Oh ho! Oh ho!

PROKHOROV: The chorus, Alyokha!

ALYOKHA: Alyokha's smokin' on his guitar,
              But nothing's coming out!
              Poom! Poom! Poom! Poom!
              So let him smoke on his guitar—
              Nothing comes out anyway!
              While I . . . (*Grinning.*) While I . . .
              I've gotta,
              I've gotta . . .

Snorting as usual, Lucy slips away to the door and bumps into Gurevich walking into the ward. He's wearing a yellow robe like everyone else, and his hair is wet. His face bears no obvious traces of a beating, but the overall bruising is quite noticeable, and everyone understands: Borenka, the delousing room.

LUCY: Oh, the new guy. Your cot's the first on
              the left. Make your own bed. I can help
              you if anything's wrong.

GUREVICH: (*vehemently*) I'll do it! Myself! Back off,
              slut!

Lucy vanishes. The singing breaks off for a while. Gurevich balls up all his linen and flings it to the corner of the bed, then looks to the right. Pink Vitya is watching him with gusto, stroking his stomach more and more lovingly, licking his lips, and sometimes turning his face into the pillow to smother a chuckle for reasons known only to him. Gurevich examines him for thirty seconds and starts to feel not so hot. He looks at his neighbor on the left. Tied up on all sides, the rear admiral is whispering something faster and faster, his face gaunt and cursed. Stasik is leaning over him.

STASIK:	Right now all the gravediggers of social-ism all over the world are confessing and taking communion. So why don't you want to, granddad?

Prokhorov is approaching. Behind him, Alyokha the Dissident, like Elisha following Elijah.

PROKHOROV:	(*to Stasik*) Hush, my delight! Let me talk with the man.
STASIK:	Oh no, he needs a minute for reflec-tion. You're not very familiar with the Orient. Well, you plunge into the water, or they plunge you, but you feel those times when you didn't exist passing out of mind—but they're washing you, therefore you do exist. When the Chi-nese emperor's concubine bathes in the Pool of the Twining Orchids—that's what it's called, the Pool of the Twining Orchids—they add twelve essences and seventeen fragrances to it.
KOLYA:	(*approaching from behind*) But anyone who cloaks himself in a yellow blanket after this, knowing neither truth nor self-restraint—he is unworthy of the yellow blanket. Can you explain this dharma to me?
PROKHOROV:	You and your dharmas can fuck off! A man's just had the living shit beaten out of him in the bath! What do dharmas have to do with it? Go on, Stas.
STASIK:	Here's the thing. I'm moving from the

bath with the orchids, passing halls of
dharmas (*glances at that lousy Kolya*)—
I'm moving from the pool to the Hall
of Perfumes, and from the Hall of Perfumes to the Hall of Canticles. On my
way, the people I meet say, "Blessed
one, go not into the mango grove." I'm
walking along, and three young women
speak to me; one is just like the moon,
another's all pastoral, wearing a dande-
lion wreath, naturally, and I don't even
look at the third. I'm sundering all bonds,
grasping all dharmas, and not aspiring
to a single delectation, so I step over the
third, pathetic lady and leave the Hall of
Canticles—for the mango grove. Eighty
thousand Himalayan elephants trail behind me. They speak to me of the vanity
of sorrow.

PROKHOROV: You know what, Stas? At least for a few
minutes, you should fuck off to your
mango groves and let me talk to the Jew.
What are you in here for, and what's your
name?

GUREVICH: Gurevich.

PROKHOROV: Gurevich. That's what I thought. But—
coincidentally—isn't it because . . . ?

He gives his throat the universal flick indicating drinking.

GUREVICH: Well, that too.

PROKHOROV: That's what I thought. Sometimes Jews
like to drink a whole lot, especially be-

hind the backs of the Arab nations. But that's not the point. As soon as a Jew shows up, any tranquillity goes out the window, and some disastrous business begins. My dear departed grandfather used to tell me a story. In the forest they had lots and lots of deer. What do you call them? Roebucks—heaps of them. And a pond filled with white swans and, on the shore of the pond, flowering rho-do-den-drons. And so a healer by the name of Gustav came to the village. I really don't know how much of a Gustav he was, but he was a Yid, that's for sure. And what came of it? This is my grandfather telling the story, not me. Before this Gustav showed up, there were so many hares in the district, you were literally tripping over them, slipping and falling on them. Then, for starters, they vanished, all the hares, and then the roebucks. No, he didn't shoot them; they went missing all by themselves. *(To Alyokha.)* Call Old Man Vova.

Vova approaches. Glancing first at Vitya, then at the rear admiral, he waits, shuddering, for the trick.

Vova, you're from the country. Try to imagine you're on the shore of a pond. You're sprouting up. Your name is Rhododendron. And on the other side of the pond, some Yid is sitting and looking at you.

VOVA:	No, I can't . . . that I'm sprouting up and—
PROKHOROV:	Oh, to hell with the damn rhododendron. Look, imagine this, Vova. You're a white swan perched on the shore of a pond, and across the way a Yid is sitting and staring at you.
VOVA:	No, I can't imagine being a white swan either. That's hard for me. I can . . . I can imagine being a flock of white swans.
PROKHOROV:	Wonderful, Vova. You're a flock of white swans, on the shore of a pond, and across the way—
VOVA:	Well, naturally, I fly off every which way. It's scary.
PROKHOROV:	Alyokha, take Vovochka away. There, you see, Gurevich?
GUREVICH:	(forcing a smile) Oh, all right.

Glances with alarm in Vitya's direction, then observes his neighbor the admiral making foolish attempts to break free of his fetters.

	Why'd this happen to him?
PROKHOROV:	Delirium tremens. He betrayed the Homeland in purpose and intent. In short, he won't drink or smoke. All that would be okay, but we were standing in the toilets and got to talking about alcohol and its awful calorie content, when this shiteater here blurts out more or less the following: "Of all the foods we swal-

low, alcohol, for all its high calorie content, has a highly primitive chemical structure and is very poor in structural information." Even then he paid for his rude erudition. I opened the window vent, squeezed him through it, and hung him upside down—and we're on the fourth—until he renounced his heretical doctrines. Today, by decision of God and the People, he's been given the death penalty. I don't really believe that in the beginning there was the Word, but there had to be some bedraggled word, and it must have been at the end, so let this bullshit artist lie there and think about that.

GUREVICH: But tell me, Prokhorov, have you been invested with authority . . . uh . . . in just this one ward or . . . ?

PROKHOROV: Of course not! Everything on that side of Vitya (*both look that way, and Gurevich turns around*)—all that is my mandated territory, but you're in luck. Tomorrow's trial is going to be intra-ward, and criminal to boot. Grisha! Remove that sheet! This is Pashka Eryomin, the Komsorg. He seems all right, your average scumbag, but it's a serious case: mutilation in the Kleinmikhel family!

Seryozha Kleinmikhel, catching his name, gets up and creeps in Prokhorov's direction.

SERYOZHA KLEINMIKHEL: Write this down. My mama had only one leg left. All the other limbs unscrewed,

her arms, too, and they were all in the
sideboard. Right then my godmother
went out for *bubliki.*

GUREVICH: Mmm, indeed. His godmother went out
for *bubliki.* What's the point of shouting?

STASIK: (*walking by as usual*) All of us have had
our godmothers go out for *bubliki.* Shout
as much as you like. No one's going to
hear you.

SERYOZHA: No, no. What do *bubliki* have to do with
this? How can you not understand? After
all, first he ripped her head off, and only
afterward—

PROKHOROV: Tomorrow, all that can keep until tomorrow. Tomorrow. Seryozha, crawl away.
Now, listen to me, Gurevich. As you see,
we have our minor ordinary absurdities.
But as it is, life with us is tolerable. They'll
give you shots for a few weeks, then pills,
then a swift kick in the ass—and off you
go. We even have a color television. A
pair of canaries. It's just today that they're
quiet. Because tomorrow's May Day.
Usually they're singing. Vitya decided
not to even touch them or take a taste,
and isn't that the highest testimonial for
a vocalist, eh, Gurevich? And over there,
higher up, near the top, there's a parrot, a
native of Hindustan, they say. And maybe
it really is from Hindustan; it must be because it hasn't said a word for days. Not a
word, not a word. But as soon as it strikes

six thirty in the morning—you'll see—it
starts, not with a twang, not metallically,
but a thousand times more parrotishly:
"Vladi-mir Sergeich! Vladi-mir Sergeich!
Get to work, work, work. Go get fucked,
fucked, fucked, fucked." And then, then
it pauses a little, for courage, and starts
in again: "Vladi-mir Sergeich! Vladimir
Sergeich! To work, work (*more and more
rapidly*), work, work, fuck, fuck, fuck,
fuck, fuck, fuck." And all this at exactly
six thirty. You can even check against the
chimes and the Kremlin stars. But there's
nothing left of the checkers and domi-
nos anymore. Vitya scarfed them down,
one by one. By a miracle, six-six survived.
Khokhulya hid it under his pillow and
played with the six-six himself, and he
always won. After a few days, something
incredible happened. Six-six disappeared
from under his pillow. Khokhulya was
beside himself, he was sobbing so, and
Vitya was smiling. It all ended with Khokhulya falling prostrate, going deaf, and
becoming a sexual mystic. Meanwhile,
Vitya's taken up chess.

*Gurevich looks, and on the nightstand in the middle of the ward
is an empty chessboard and, on it, a white queen.*

STASIK: (*jumping up*) And he's tucked it all away!
                                 Why has he only taken pity on the white
                                 queen? He's got real nerve; he ate the
                                 time-out, and the queen's gambit, and
                                 the Sicilian defense.

PROKHOROV: Here's what, Vitya (*sitting next to Vitya on the bed*). Vitya, you've eaten all the board games. Tell me, you ate them simply out of moral considerations, right? Did they seem too reckless to you? I have a doctor with me from the center.

Points to Gurevich.

And oh what a doctor he is!

Points up.

He's wondering why you eat so much. Don't you have enough fodder and provisions?

Vitya can't tolerate the monitor's glance, stops stroking his belly, hides shyly behind his sleeve.

VITYA: It tastes good. *lol*

PROKHOROV: But why did you take pity on the white queen? Eh?

VITYA: I felt sorry for her. She's so lonely.

PROKHOROV: I understand. And tell me, Vitenka, are eats all you dream of?

VITYA: No, no. The tsarevna . . .

PROKHOROV: The tsarevna? The dead one?

VITYA: No, the live tsarevna. She's the cat's meow with that blue bow. Like Cinderella. And the prince keeps walking around her and keeps hitting her over the head with the glass slipper.

PROKHOROV:	And would you eat that glass slipper? (*Points.*) Chow-Chow!
STASIK:	You shouldn't call him Vitya. You should call him Nina. Nina Chow-Chow-Adze.
VITYA:	I would, just to keep him from hitting her.
GUREVICH:	Well, and if the tsarevna is dead — that is, if he's beaten her? To death? Would you eat the dead tsarevna?
VITYA:	(*smiles*) Yes.
GUREVICH:	What if she had seven superheroes with her? Then what?
VITYA:	I'd eat the seven superheroes, too.
GUREVICH:	Well, what about thirty-three super-heroes?
VITYA:	Yes. If the nurses didn't rush me, of course.
GUREVICH:	But . . . Listen up. What about twenty-eight Panfilov heroes?
VITYA:	(*with the same carefree and terrible smile*) Yes. (*Dreaming.*)
GUREVICH:	(*persistently*) But twenty-six Baku com-missars? Them, too?
PROKHOROV:	(*breaks into the discussion*) Well, that's it. Tomorrow we'll have Komsorg Pashka for you, too. What do you care? You refused the admiral — I understand you. Admirals are too crunchy, but real Komsorgs, now, they never crunch. Seryozha! Klein-

mikhel! Come over here. Tell me, did
you notice traces of the slightest remorse
on the criminal's face?

SERYOZHA: No, I didn't. And that day my dear departed mother winked at me: "Keep an
eye on Pashka," she said. If he'd been the
least bit ashamed that he was naughty
with me like that—but no, he wasn't. He
spent the whole evening afterward booz-
ing the vodka and hooliganing the disci-
pline. And he forbade me to air the house
out using the window so there wouldn't
be a whiff of Mama left.

STASIK: (*passing by, as usual*) Still, it's nice living
in an age of universal decay. There's just
one bad thing. Man shouldn't have had
his lymph glands removed. The fact that
he had the *bubliki* and pickles taken
away isn't so bad. And that they took
away his melon is nonsense; you can sur-
vive without melons, too. We don't need
plebiscites, either. But at least let's keep
our lymph glands.

*While Stasik was orating, both doors to Ward 3 were flung open,
and on the threshold Male Nurse Borenka and Nurse Aide Tamarochka appeared. They neither of them look at the patients so much
as spit at them with their eyes. Both understand that their mere appearance induces instant catalepsy and grief—and there's plenty of
that as is—in all the wards.*

PROKHOROV: Up! Everyone, up! Rounds!

*Everyone stands up slowly except Khokhulya, Old Man Vova,
and Gurevich.*

Under Borya the Goon's lab coat is a well-brushed chocolate-brown suit, and topping his tight shirt is a tie around his fat neck. Hardly anyone has ever seen him in this raiment. It's just that today he's the duty nurse on May Day Eve. He jokingly steps toward Stasik, who has frozen in his saluting-arm pose.

BORYA THE GOON:	So, you fucking bitch, you mean you're missing some glands?
TAMARA:	Quit farting around, boy, you're just about to get all your glands put right where they belong.

Borya, playing, gives Stas a lightning jab to the solar plexus, and Stas drops, writhing, to the floor.

	(*pointing to Vova*) And this shitty shrimp, why isn't he getting up? Why's he disobeying orders?
BORYA:	We'll have to ask him that. Vovochka, any complaints?
VOVA:	No, no complaints about my health at all. It's just I really want to go home. The lungwort's blooming there now. April's nearly over. At home, when you come down the front steps, there's a whole glade of lungwort edge to edge, and the bees are all over it by now.
BORYA:	(*straightening his tie*) Nina, I'm a city man, and your lungworts mean nothing to me. What color are they, Vovochka?
VOVA:	Well, how can I tell you? They're dark blue and sky blue. Oh, like the sky after sunset in late April.

Borya sinks his nails into the tip of Vova's nose and gives it a few twists as Tamarochka laughs. Vova's nose turns the color of April lungwort. Vova weeps.

BORYA:
(*continuing rounds*) How are we breathing, Khokhulya? Igor Lvovich's coming to see you in five minutes with a dandy instrument, and you're going to have to do a little bending. What about you, Kolya?

KOLYA:
I have a complaint. I don't know how many years I've been on this ward. Because they told me I'm an Estonian, and my head hurts. But I haven't been an Estonian for a long time, and my head stopped hurting a long time ago, but they keep holding me and holding me.

Tamarochka is meanwhile drawn to the spectacle on her right: Seryozha Kleinmikhel, turned toward the window, is quietly praying.

TAMAROCHKA:
Ah! At it again, you nutcase!

Puffing her gray cheeks, she heads toward him.

How many times do I have to teach you? First, the right shoulder, and after that, the left. Here, look!

She grabs him by the scruff of his neck, spits in his face, punches him in the forehead, and takes a big swing at his right shoulder, then at his left, then under the ribs.

Should I repeat that?

She repeats the same thing once again, only with more force and a cheerful bravado.

	Shit on a brick! If I see you crossing your-self one more time, I'm going to drown you in the slop pail!
BORYA:	Quit it, Tamarochka, quit soiling your hands. Why don't you come over here?

Flinging Kolya aside, he moves toward the admiral, Vitya, and Gurevich. He's followed by his entourage: the monitor Prokhorov, Alyokha the Dissident, and Tamarochka.

PROKHOROV:	As you see, the comrade rear admiral cannot stand before you at attention. Punished for being violent and for his corrupt spyingness. Or rather, for his spying corruptness and unruliness.
BORYA:	I see, I see.

The corner of his eye slides over Gurevich, who is pensively chewing his nails, and passes on to Vitya. Vitya, with his pink smile, is happily ensconced in his cot, dealt out like solitaire.

TAMAROCHKA:	Hello, Vitenka, hello, my treasure.

With an open palm, she up and slaps Vitya on the belly. Vitya's smile disappears.

	How are things with our digestion, Vitenka dear?
VITYA:	That hurt.
BORYA:	(*guffaws along with Tamarochka*) What about our other esteemed patients? Don't they hurt, too? Here they are all chorus-ing to go home. And why, Vityusha? It's very simple. You've caused them pain;

you've taken away their intellectual diversions. Take a look at all those ugly, suffering faces. So here's the thing. Let's agree, today . . .

TAMAROCHKA: Today, after you go about your shitting, all the board games have to be where they belong. Otherwise, we'll have to have a postmortem. And you know very well, my dear, that we don't do postmortems on the living, just on corpses.

Prokhorov, meanwhile, is watching Alyokha the Dissident with alarm. But more about that a little later.

Borya, spreading his chocolate-trousered legs and crossing his arms, stands over the sitting Gurevich.

BORYA: Up!

TAMAROCHKA: Why isn't this dirty Yid's bed made yet?

BORYA: (*just as quietly*) Up.

Gurevich remains self-absorbed. Quiet all around.

(*raising Gurevich's chin with one little finger*) Up!

Gurevich meekly rises and — taking everyone by surprise — with a brief shout plunges his fist into Borenka's jaw. There are a few seconds of silence, if you don't count Tamarochka's screech. Borenka, not affected in any way, cold-bloodedly, grabs Gurevich, lifts him into the air, and with all his strength brings him crashing down onto the floor, maneuvering him so he hits his side against the edge of the iron bed. Then two or three kicks in the vicinity of his liver, just to be a wiseass.

	(*to Tamarochka*) Prepare the sulfo for the patient. I'll give him the shot myself.
PROKHOROV:	What are you going to do, Boris? He's new here. It's the delirium of justice seeking, the sense of falsely understood honor, and other atavisms.
BORYA:	Why don't you shut up? Ass.

The men in white coats move away.

PROKHOROV:	Alyokha!
ALYOKHA:	Yes, here I am.
PROKHOROV:	First aid to all victims of the raid! Stasik, get up. It's okay. They fucked off. Nothing extraordinary. The best is yet to come. First, Gurevich.

Prokhorov and Alyokha, with Kolya's feeble assistance, drag Gurevich, who is barely breathing, to the bed, cover him with blankets, and sit down around him.

	Fine people, these Jews, fine people. Here's the only trouble, though. They have no idea how to live. Now they're going to give him the works. That's for sure. (*In a whisper.*) Gu-re-vich.
GUREVICH:	(*moans a little and can barely speak*) It's okay. They won't give me the works. I'm getting a present ready for them, too.
PROKHOROV:	(*delighted that Gurevich is alive and functioning*) A May Day present. That's splendid. Only first they have to give you one, see, in about five minutes.

Make you laugh, Gurevich, before your
minor torture? My loyal confidant Alyokha will make them pay. You know
how he became a dissident? I'll tell you.
You do know that every Russian vil-
lage has its idiot. What kind of a Rus-   *holy fool?*
sian village is it without its village idiot?
People would look at that village as they
would at a Britain that still didn't have
a single Constitution. So look. Alyokha
walked around, completely zonked out,
in Pavlovo-Posad. He'd sweep the train
station square a little, help with loading.
But he had a fiery passion inside that remains to this day. You see, our Alyokha is
a giant when it comes to physiognomism.
Just one glance from him at any sorry-
ass face and he knows exactly where the
jackass should go and in what capacity.
The foolproof irritant for him was this:
thorough ironing and a tie. What would
he do? Nothing. He'd steal up on his victim, though not too close, give his nose
a good squeeze—and there it was, his
booger hanging off that tie. The whole
town called him a dissident. They were
stunned by his impunity, and the novelty
of his struggle against the existing order
of things, and his subordination. Two
months ago they hauled him in here.

GUREVICH: Marvelous. However much I contem-
plate our nation and what it wants . . .
this is exactly what it needs . . . without
all the rest. . . . It's going to make it.

PROKHOROV:	And precision! Precision, Gurevich! The great Leonardo, the rumors say, was no fool when it came to ballistics. But he can't compare to Alyokha! Alyokha!
ALYOKHA:	I've been here the whole time.
PROKHOROV:	Well, that's just terrific. Alyokha, don't you find that your method of struggle with world evil is, well, rather unappetizing? We all realize you can't do business in white gloves, but how did you decide that if the gloves aren't bloody, then they have to be covered in shit, snot, or vomit? You should read those left-wingers less. Those cute Italians.
ALYOKHA:	Heaven forbid. I only read Marshal Vasilievsky. Even so, they say the marshal made a mistake: he should have gone from west to east, not east to west.
PROKHOROV:	(*trying to buck up Gurevich before his torture*) Modern dissidence, in the person of Alyokha, loses sight of the fact that first you have to pull it out by the root— and later all the rest will come out with the same rotten root. Our streets and squares need changing. Judge for yourself. They have the Bridge of Sighs, the rue Sainte Geneviève, the Boulevard of Obscure Languor, and so on, while we have—well, list the streets of your district. The soul withers at the sound. For starters you have to say Capital Street— in the middle, naturally—and parallel

to it is Jubilee Street, all busts and pop-
lars. It's all crossed and overshadowed by
Special Moscow Street. Running off in
fright from its beauty in all directions are
Pepper, Ginger, Streltsy, Don Steppe,
Old Russia, and Sagebrush. These, naturally, are connected by the lanes: Des-
sert, Brut, Demi-Sec, Sweet, and Demi-
Doux. And then there are the bridges
thrown across all this: Strong White, For-
tified Rosé — what's the difference? And
at their foot, the hotels — Benedictine,
Chartreuse — rise along the embank-
ment, and down below, the gentlemen
and their ladies stroll, the gentlemen
looking at the ladies and the clouds, and
the ladies at the clouds and the gentlemen, and all of them throwing dust in
the eyes of the nations of Europe while
the nations of Europe shake off the dust.

*Once again the ward doors are flung open. The hospital's head
physician, Igor Lvovich Raninson. Behind him, Male Nurse Borya,
holding a syringe. The syringe doesn't surprise anyone. Everyone is
looking at the peculiar suitcase Raninson is holding.*

BORYA: Over there.

*He points out Khokhulya to Raninson. Raninson is impene-
trable. So is Khokhulya. Laying out his box of electrodes, Raninson
examines the patient disdainfully. Khokhulya doesn't look at the
doctor at all; he has plenty of thoughts of his own.*

                                (*approaching Gurevich's bed*) Well, now.
                                Prokhorov, turn the patient over and bare
                                his buttock.

GUREVICH:	I'll . . . my-s-s-self

Turns over on his belly with a moan; Alyokha and Prokhorov help him. Borya, without the slightest malevolence, but also not without a show of omnipotence, stands with the syringe held vertically, spurting it a little; then he leans over and plants the injection.

BORYA:	Cover him up.
PROKHOROV:	He needs a second blanket. Overnight his temperature shot up past forty. I do know. . . .
BORYA:	No blankets. It's not indicated. And if he gets too hot, he can walk around and breathe. If he can stir just his one left . . . Gurevich! If you don't take a turn for the better from the sulfazine tonight, I want you to come see me at supper. Or rather, at the May Day rally. Your weakness, Natalia Alexeyevna, will be laying the table herself. Well, how about it?
GUREVICH:	(*with great effort*) I will.
BORYA:	(*guffaws but completely misses the fact that Alyokha the Dissident is approaching with one finger on his nostril*) But today we're being hospitable. Me especially. We'll treat you like family, encrust you with gems.
GUREVICH:	I . . . I . . . I said I would. I'll come.

Alyokha fires his right nostril, and skillfully. The ward is deafened by a scream the likes of which no one on the ward has ever heard. Doctor Raninson has performed his high-volt trick on Khokhulya, poor devil.

BORYA: (*grabbing Alyokha the Dissident by the
                                throat*) I'll deal with you—later. You
                                know what, Alyoshenka? Igor Lvovich
                                here . . . as soon as he leaves, you and
                                I are going to have a good blow, okay?
                                (*Wipes his tie with his handkerchief.*)

*Raninson, walking through the ward with his diabolical case,
surveys the patients: each physiognomy except for Prokhorov's and
Alyokha's bears the seal of eternity—but definitely not the eternity
we are all looking forward to.*

RANINSON: A happy holiday of international soli-
                                darity for all you workers, comrade
                                patients. Come with me, Boris Anatolie-
                                vich. I need you.

They leave.

PROKHOROV: (*who, as soon as the white coats dis-
                                appear, hangs on the neck of Alyokha the
                                Dissident*) Alyokha! You Hyperborean
                                you! You Alcibiades! You Emerald! You
                                really are Murat riding a white horse
                                onto the Arbat! You're Farabundo Martí!
                                No, the Russian nation does not want
                                for zealots, and it never will! You be the
                                judge. Before the Yasnaya Polyana count
                                could peg out, Comrade Kokkinaki was
                                already lying there in diapers, and he
                                already had wings! In 1921, Alexander
                                Blok cast off—nothing you can do about
                                that, we're all mortal, even Blok. And so?
                                Exactly a year and a half later, the im-
                                mortal Zoya Kosmodemyanskaya is born!

GUREVICH:	(*half rising on an elbow approvingly*) Quite true, monitor.
ALYOKHA:	(*elated*) I should have fired away at Igor Lvovich a little, too.
PROKHOROV:	Come off it, knight! That would have been going overboard. Let's not go complicating the plot of the drama now in progress with minor subplots. Am I right in saying that, Gurevich? Humanity doesn't need any more deductive detectives; humanity is sick of racy plots.
GUREVICH:	You can't imagine just how sick. And why cook up these plots with them? After all, essentially they don't exist. We're the psychos, and those phantasmagorias in white, they appear to us periodically. It's sickening, of course, but what can we do? So they appear, and they disappear, and make themselves out to be full of joie de vivre.
PROKHOROV:	True, true, and Borya and Tamarochka laugh and neck to assure us they're the genuine article and certainly not our chimeras and delusions — not figments at all.
GUREVICH:	Come over here. Prokhorov, regarding chimeras, this here (*points to the injection site*) — is this going to hurt long?
PROKHOROV:	Hurt? Ha ha. "Hurt" isn't the word. You're going to start feeling it in an hour or an hour and a half. Three or four days from now, maybe, you'll be able to move

your legs. It's okay, Gurevich. It'll resolve itself. I'll distract you the best I can. I'll sing you Comrade Raukhverger's children's songs and, oh, Oskar Feltsman's, Frenkel's, Lev Knipper's, and Daniil Pokrass's — basically everything to the words of Simeon Lazarevich Shulman, Inna Goff, and Solomon Fogelson.

GUREVICH: Prokhorov, I beg of you.

PROKHOROV: Don't beg of me, Gurevich. Alyokha and I will carry you over to the color television. Evgeny Iosifovich Gabrilovich, Alexei Yakovlevich Kapler, Heifitz and Romm, Ermler, Stolper and Fainzimmer. Sulamif Moiseyevna Tsybulnik. In short, the pains in your hipbone will subside. And if they don't, at your service will be Volkenshtein, Kriger, Grebner, and Kreps — no better fellow anywhere, but why did he start collaborating with Gendelshtein?

GUREVICH: Tell me, Prokhorov, is there any pain reliever for this sulfo shot? Other than Fainzimmer and Sulamif Moiseyevna Tsybulnik?

PROKHOROV: Easy as pie. A stiff shot of vodka. Pure alcohol — even better. (*Whispers something into Gurevich's ear.*)

GUREVICH: And that's for sure?

PROKHOROV: At any rate, Natalie's replacing the duty nurse today. She's got all the keys, Gure-

	vich. She doesn't even entrust them to Borenka the Goon, her *bel ami*.
GUREVICH:	(*stiffening, tries to stand*) Now here's something. (*He stiffens again at the audacity of it all.*) I have an idea.
PROKHOROV:	I can guess what idea it is.
GUREVICH:	Oh, no, much more audacious than you're thinking. I'm going to blow them up tonight!
NURSE LUCY'S VOICE:	(*from behind the door*) Shot time, boys! Boys! The treatment room, for your shots!

No one in Ward 3 pays any attention. Gurevich alone takes tentative steps.

GUREVICH:	(*whispers something to Prokhorov*)

> Yes, I'll be back. In fifteen, more or
>   less.
> Crowned or crippled. It's all the
>   same.

PROKHOROV:	Bravo! You are a poet, Gurevich!
GUREVICH:	

> If only! Wish me luck. Though they
>   may well
> Carry me in on a shield, with a
>   shiner
> For my trouble . . . but I'll lay ten to
>   one,
> I'll be carrying the shield—and no
>   shiner.

Curtain.

ACT THREE

Lyrical intermezzo. The treatment room. Natalie, sitting in a cushy chair, is scribbling on some papers. In the next room, the Aminazine room, which is separated from the treatment room by a screen, is the silent line for shots, and the only voice from there is Tamarochka's. She sounds more or less like this: "All the shots in the ass I've given you! And you go on and on like a fool! Next! Hurts? Oh, and I really believe you! Cut the crap, you mama's boy! Who do you think you are, asking me for aspirin? Quite the von baron you are! He needs aspirin! Even going easy, you'll pop off anyway! Aspirin or no. Who needs you anyway, asshole? Next!" Natalie is so used to this, she doesn't flinch, let alone listen. She's buried in her big fat reports. A knock at the door.

GUREVICH:	*(wearily)* Natalie?
NATALIE:	I knew you'd come again, Gurevich. But what's the matter?
GUREVICH:	I'm a little beat. But Tasso's back at Leonora's feet!
NATALIE:	But why's this Tasso limping?
GUREVICH:	Why don't you understand? Your dimwit

why do they start speaking in iambs?

Goon—he hasn't forgotten
    anything.
No sooner did you walk into
    admitting
Than immediately I noticed that he
    noticed
Immediately that . . .

NATALIE: What dimwit? What Goon?
What does Borka have to do with
    this?
To fill a moron with so much tittle-
    tattle
In just two hours! Gurevich, dear
    man,
Come here, you silly . . .

Finally, an embrace. Gurevich looks over her shoulder at the door.

How many years have you been
    gone, you blockhead?

GUREVICH: You know how we measure time—
The other sickos and me. (*Tenderly.*)
Natalia . . .

NATALIE: What is it, dummy? I barely
    recognized you.
'Fess up: you've been drinking
    something fierce.

GUREVICH: Oh no, just a drop from time to
    time.

NATALIE: And your hands, Lev, why've they
    got the shakes?

GUREVICH:	Oh, my dear, why don't you understand?
	My hand shakes—so be it. How does vodka enter
	Into it? Hands shake when the soul is homeless,

Points to himself.

Inspired, malnourished, or angry,
When the heart is weary, or filled
    with dread
Over ruinous passions or a meeting
    long craved,

Natalie smiles faintly.

And finally, for love of the
    Fatherland.
No, not "finally"! Above all—
The presence of such a divinity,
Where the dimple, and bust, and—

NATALIE:	(*covers his mouth with her hand*) Well, aren't you just the chatterbox now. Why don't I put a little glucose in you. You're all dried out and gloomy.
GUREVICH:	Isn't that because of you, Natalie?
NATALIE:	Ha ha! How I ever believed you.

Gets up, takes a key chain out of the right pocket of her white coat and opens a cupboard. Fiddles around for a long time with the ampoules, test tubes, and syringes. Gurevich, biting his nails as usual, can't take his eyes off the keys or Natalie's bewitching movements.

GUREVICH:	Look what they write: on the small marine amphipod, the eyes take up nearly one-third of the entire body. More or less the same as on you. But the other two-thirds are getting me more worked up today for some reason. And also that triumphant pin in your hair.

> You're pure, as pure as profit. Like
>   the dew
> On the petals of something or
>   other.
> Like—

NATALIE:	Why don't you hush up.

Approaches him with a syringe.

> Don't be afraid, Lev, I won't hurt you hardly at all; you won't even notice.

She starts the treatment, and the glucose is quietly injected. He and she watch each other.

TAMAROCHKA'S VOICE:	(*from the other side of the screen*) Just why are you hollering like a stuck pig? The person in front of you—I just stuck him—and he couldn't give a rat's ass. Next! What's this? Change what pillow-case now? Eat dirt, buddy. You! You un-washed prick! Did you see the pile of garbage by the kitchen? Well, tomorrow we're going to bury smart alecks like you there and cart you out in trucks. Next!
NATALIE:	A penny for your thoughts, Gurevich. Ignore her. Look at me.

GUREVICH:	That's what I'm doing. Only I was thinking about how humanity is degenerating headlong anyway. From the resplendent Queen Tamar to this Tamarochka here. From Francisco Goya to his fellow tribesman and namesake General Franco. From Gaius Julius Caesar to César Cui—and from him all the way to Tsezar Solodar. From Korolenko the humanist to Krylenko the prosecutor. Why Korolenko anyway? Immanuel Kant to "Steppe Supplicant." Vitus Bering to Hermann Goering. David the psalm singer to David Tukhmanov. And . . .
NATALIE:	(*screws in some new crap to go into the same needle and resumes injecting something else*) And what about you, Lev? Are you better than the previous Levs? What do you think?
GUREVICH:	Not better, but different from the previous Levs. Here's what happened to me: We were the least bit snockered, and we were standing in the cold and waiting for—God knows what we were waiting for, but that's not the point. The main thing is that all three of my random friends were streaming steam from their mouths—no surprise in the freezing cold! But I wasn't. And they noticed. They asked, "Why is it freezing cold, and you don't have steam coming out of anywhere? Come on, breathe out again!" I breathed out, and again no steam. All

	three said, "Something's wrong here. We have to inform the proper authorities."
NATALIE:	(*giggles*) Did they?
GUREVICH:	Did they ever. I was summoned immediately to a clinic or dispensary, and they asked me only one question: "What's the reason for your steam?" I told them, "That's the thing. I don't have any steam." And they said, "No, no. Answer the question. On what basis do you have steam?" If they'd asked, say, René Descartes this question, he would simply have collapsed into the Russian snowdrifts and said nothing. But I said, "Take me to the 126th Police Precinct. I have something to tell them about Cornelius Sulla." So they did.
NATALIE:	You went and blabbed about Sulla? Did they understand anything?
GUREVICH:	Not a damn thing, but they took me to the 126th. They asked, "Are you Gurevich?" "Yes," I said, "Gurevich.

> I'm here suspected of
>   superhumanhood.
> And up to a point you're perfectly
>   right:
> Yes, yes. I'm superhuman, and
>   nothing
> Superhuman is alien to me.
> Like Napoleon, I cannot swim.
> I do not comb my hair, like
>   Beethoven.

I know no languages, just like
      Chapaev.
Unproductive am I, like Vespucci or
Copernicus: forty pages, maybe
      forty-eight
In his whole a-normous age.
I'm like Saint Anthony of Padua.
I haven't washed my feet for months,
      or cut
My nails, like Hölderlin, the
      German poet.
For weeks at a time—no, no, make
      that years—
I haven't changed my shirt, just like
      that
Archduchess Isabella, damn her eyes,
Albrecht's wife, the Austrian.
      However,
She vowed: 'Until east India's
      triumph,
My clothes I, too, will not change.'
I, too, vow not to don a single shirt
Until the final anti-Bolshevik
Flees to the West and purifies the
      air!
You see, I am akin to all the greats.
But unlike King Philip number two,
The Spaniard, I do not have mange.
Now that's the truth. (*Sigh.*) But I do
      have lice,
Which were abundantly bestowed
      upon
Cornelius Sulla, sovereign of Rome.
Am I free to go?"

	"You are," they told me, "of course you are. We'll take you home right now in our car." And they brought me here.
NATALIE:	What about the Young Communist City Committee spire?
GUREVICH:	Oh, that was a diversion, to get you in the admitting room to lighten up.
NATALIE:	Listen, Lev, do you want a little drink? Only shh!
GUREVICH:	Oh, Natalie! My whole being cries out For resurrection, not for courage.

While Natalie pours something and dilutes it with water from the tap, there's no letup behind the screen.

TAMAROCHKA'S VOICE:	Shit on a brick, friend, it's not so bad! Be a man, you half-sour cunt! Next! And your pants, how many pants have you put on? All nuts rot and fall off eventually! Come on, come on! And you—back the fuck off, quit getting in my way. Next! It's okay, old man, you're on the mend. You'll be going around like that, bowlegged, for another couple weeks, and then—shit, if you don't! We're only three hundred meters from the morgue! Next!

Natalie offers Gurevich a glass. He drinks slowly and then presses his lips to Natalie's hand gratefully.

GUREVICH:	She has a psyche, crude and beastly— Thus Heraclitus of Ephesus once spoke.

NATALIE:	Who's that you're talking about?
GUREVICH:	This is all still about Tamarochka, our sister of mercy. You've noticed how moral principles are deteriorating in the Russian nation. Even in the Baltics. Before, when there was a sudden pause in the middle of a conversation, a Russian muzhik usually said, "The angel of silence just flew over." Now when that happens: "A policeman kicked the bucket somewhere!" Whenever it thunders, a muzhik always crosses himself—that's how it was before. But now it's: "Until the roast cock pecks him in the ass." Or remember this one? "All ages bow down to love." But now it's just: "A prick isn't looking for others its age." Ho ho. Or, there's this one—very touching, really: "For a sweetheart, seven versts is a drop in the bucket." Listen to how it is now: "For a mad dog, a hundred kiluometers is a quick trip to the store."

Natalie laughs.

> Here's another, even cleaner. The old Russian saying "Don't spit in the well; a good drink may come in handy"—it's been transformed: "Don't piss in the pudding; that's where the cook washes his feet."

Natalie is laughing so hard the screen is moved aside and through it pokes sister of mercy Tamarochka's face.

TAMAROCHKA:	Oho! Not a day passes without a new suitor for Natalia Alexeyevna! Today, one handsomer than all the rest put together. A dirty Yid and psycho both—two points in his favor.
NATALIE:	(*calming the rebellious Gurevich, sternly addresses Tamarochka*) After this shift, Tamara Makarovna, you and I are going to have a talk. But right now, I have things to do.

Tamarochka goes back, and it all starts up again.

TAMAROCHKA'S VOICE:	(*from the other side of the screen*) What do you mean! Give him a sleeping pill and you'll get fuckall. Stop shaking! The slightest peep out of you, shithead! (*And so forth.*)
NATALIE:	Lev, dear man, calm yourself (*kisses him and then kisses him again*)—it's going to be different, you'll see. Anyway, it's no good getting worked up. After all, the patients here, who are the majority, don't have the right to answer insult for insult. To say nothing—God forbid—of blow for blow. You can't even cry here—did you know that? They'll give you a shot, smother you with neuroleptics, for just one wail. Have you ever had occasion to cry even a little, Lev?
GUREVICH:	Ho! There was a time when I made my living doing that.

NATALIE:	Made your living with tears? I don't understand.
GUREVICH:	It's actually very simple. During my student years, for example. Oy, I can't help it: back to iambs again.

> Did you know I used to weep,
>   Natalie?
> Not for any reason. But on
>   command.
> The whole wide world soon found
>   out I could.
> They would say, "Weep, Gurevich,
>   weep!"
> Amid Bacchic, oh, and other
>   matters:
> "Weep, Gurevich, weep a flood of
>   tears."
> And so I wept. Half a ruble per flood.
> Do you—do you understand,
>   Natalie?
> At the drop of a hat! On any
>   command!
> The tears—the anguish—
>   completely genuine!
> I, a loud adolescent, never guessed
> That there was human, even Jewish
>   grief.
> Titanic grief. And so it is.
> Of other tears I do not speak.

NATALIE:	You know what else, Gurevich. Avoid speaking in iambic pentameter—especially with the doctors. They think you're mocking them. They'll start treat-

ing you with sulfazine or something even
harsher. Come, please, for my sake, don't.

GUREVICH: Lord! So why am I here? That's what
I don't understand. And the other
patients—them, too—why are they?

> They're all just fine, these people of
> yours,
> Mollusks, cephalopods, and
> children,
> They've slipped slightly into
> oblivion.
> Not one of them would imagine
> he is
> A hundred-watt lightbulb, or a
> sidewalk,
> Or the thaw in the early days of
> March,
> A muezzin, the Tower of Pisa,
> Or the Jackson-Fulbright
> Amendment to
> Resolutions of the U.S. Congress.
> Not even Comet Schwassmann-
> Wachman 1.
> Why am I here if I'm strong as an
> ox?

NATALIE: Listen up, Fulbright, you're alive
until
You're sick. But after that? What's not
To understand, Gurevich? Viruses,
germs—
One look and they frown and turn
away.

GUREVICH: Bravo. Filled with wonders, mighty na-
                 ture is, as Comrade Berendei once said.
                 Only the thing is, I could get along per-
                 fectly well without all of you. Except for
                 you, of course, Natalie. You be the judge.
                 A luxurious infirmary all to myself, a
                 shot of piracetam in the butt all to my-
                 self. I could be my own informer, and the
                 whistle in his teeth, too. I could be fire
                 and fire chief both.

NATALIE: Gurevich, dear man, you have let your-
                 self go a little.

GUREVICH: What does that mean? Say it's true. Com-
                 pared with how much I've been through
                 and how much has gone by—I haven't
                 let myself go very far! Our nation's great
                 Volga River flows for thirty-seven hun-
                 dred kilometers, during which time it
                 lets itself go down just 221 meters. *Brock-
                 haus Encyclopedia.* I'm all about the
                 Brockhaus Encyclopedia. Only I didn't
                 get a good-enough look—and accidently
                 incinerated a stack of this, that, and the
                 other. But I haven't let myself go at all.
                 Every body, even a heavenly body (*sur-
                 veys all of Natalie significantly*)—well,
                 even a heavenly body has its own per-
                 sonal vortexes. René Descartes. How
                 many of my own vortexes have I inciner-
                 ated in myself, how many pure and meek
                 impulses? How many maids of Orléans
                 have I burned inside me? How many pal-
                 lid Desdemonas have I smothered? And

	how many Mumus and Chapaevs have I drowned inside me!
NATALIE:	You're an extraordinary troublemaker!!
GUREVICH:	I'm not extraordinary. Just intense. Yet today as well, yes, I'm nearly set. I'll start not to let myself go—to fall. This very night I'll rip up to shreds The tragedy, the iamb ban. In short, I'll blow this place to little pieces!
	Especially since—and this I've completely forgotten—it's May Day Eve. The night of Walpurgis, Saint Wedekind's sister. Since the late eighth century, this night has always been marked by something terrifying and wonderworking. Involving Satan. I don't know whether or not there'll be a witches' sabbath today, but something is going to happen.
NATALIE:	Oh, Levushka, don't scare me. I'm on duty all night tonight.
GUREVICH:	Paired with your nice friend Borenka? The Goon?

NATALIE:	Yes, imagine. My most gracious
	    friend.
	And the very purest alcohol.
	There'll be cakes I made myself and
	    the songs
	Of the immortal Iosif Kobzon.
	And so it goes, ex-sweetheart, my
	    ex-mine!

GUREVICH:	I don't remember exactly which realm it is, Natalie, where they spank a lady with a bouquet of blue gillyflowers for jokes like that, but if you like, I can glorify you — in the style of Nikolai Nekrasov, of course.
NATALIE:	Go on, glorify me, silly.
GUREVICH:	À la Nikolai Nekrasov!

> Roman said, "What big eyes!"
> Demian said, "What big tits!"
> Luka said, "She'll do."
> "And a sturdy fanny, too,"
> said the Gubin brothers,
> Ivan and Mitrodor.
> Old Man Pakhom buckled down
> And prayed, an eye cast to the
>   ground:
> "That fanny came easy to you!
> Just so she has a good soul."
> And Prov said, "Ho ho!"

Natalie claps.

> Meanwhile, you know, Natalie, the amusing and precise way Nekrasov defined a Russian woman's degree of attractiveness? Here's how he defined it: by the number of men who wouldn't mind giving her a pinch. Right now I'd be more than happy to give you a pinch.

NATALIE:	Well, pinch away if you like. Only cut the banalities. And take it easy, silly.
GUREVICH:	What banalities? When a man wants to convince himself he's not sleeping but

	has woken up, he has to pinch himself, vulgar man that he is.
NATALIE:	Of course he does. But himself. Not a lady standing however close.
GUREVICH:	What's the difference? Ah, you're standing very close. Natalie the tormenter. When you sway at the waist like that, I can't help it—I feel like grabbing you from behind and making sparks shower down in front of you.
NATALIE:	Pooh! You booby. Go ahead, then. Grab away!

Gurevich does just that. Natalie, her head thrown back. A never-ending kiss. what

GUREVICH:	Oh, Natalie! Let me catch my breath! I even have this strong memory—three years ago you were wearing that foxy little dress. Why was I the only one driven to those Kunluns? I became a philosopher. I imagined that black lust had ceased to be my life's dominant note at last. Now I know for sure that there is no black lust. No black sin. Only the human lot can be black.
NATALIE:	Why is it, Gurevich, that you drink so much but know absolutely everything?
GUREVICH:	Natalie!
NATALIE:	I'm listening, silly. What else do you want, you dimwit?

GUREVICH: Natalie.

*He embraces her violently and locks eyes with her. Meanwhile
his hands—moved by passion, naturally—roam convulsively over
Natalie's hips and pubic articulation. The viewer can see her yellow
key chain transferring from the pocket of Natalie's white coat to Gurevich's hospital robe. The kiss continues.*

NATALIE: (*a little later*) I've missed you, Gurevich.
                        (*Slyly.*) How's your Lucy?

GUREVICH: I ran away from her, Natalie. What is
                        Lucy really? I told her, "Don't be born
                        peevish." She told me, "Drop dead, you
                        miserable triumvir!" Why "triumvir" I
                        still don't know. Afterward, chasing after
                        me: "You'll come to a rotten end, Gure-
                        vich! You'll drink yourself off a cliff, like
                        Kollontai in Stockholm! You'll die in the
                        gutter, like Klim Voroshilov!"

NATALIE: (*laughs*) But which first?

GUREVICH: Which does come first? Please don't
                                    reminisce.
                        Natalie! She taunted me, reluctant
                        As I was to rest my body on hers,
                        To lay it down like a cool celestial
                                    ray
                        Resting on autumn's new-mown
                                    field, the way
                        A brow lies down on a serious
                                    thought.
                        Bah! A thought on his . . .
                        Forget about Lucy. Did you miss
                                    me?

	But you threw that hussy in my face To make the Goon legitimate, right?
NATALIE:	Again! You should be ashamed of yourself!

GUREVICH:	No, I'm well read, of that you're
	    convinced.
	And so today, on the eve of May Day,
	I'll come and you'll let two hundred
	    grams go
	Missing. Not by fluke. Or without
	    his leave:
	Your Borenka invited me, and I
	Said I would come. I nodded my
	    assent.

NATALIE:	You do realize, though, don't you?

GUREVICH:	I do.
	There's who to go Don Juaning with,
	    curse him!
	The Goon and you—it's more than
	    I can bear.
	Oh, come dawn, that big fat hog is
	    going
	To hear steps—the Commander's
	    steps!

NATALIE:	Gurevich, dear man, you've lost your mind.

GUREVICH:	Not a bit—quite yet. Oh, have it
	    your way:
	Like the sky's edge I will flicker,
	    flicker,
	If you ask me to . . .

Thinks about that.

	If you ask me to I will blaze like the edge of the sky! 'Til I go entirely off my rocker. Just wait until Act 5 — then we shall see. Natalia, dear girl . . .
NATALIE:	What, you nincompoop?

GUREVICH:	If you wore thirty thousand
	    dresses — more!
	If you'd only a cross between your
	    breasts
	And nothing else at all — I would
	    still —

NATALIE:	(*covering his mouth with her palm for the umpteenth time; tenderly*) Ah! You remember that, too, awful man!

Someone coughs on the other side of the door.

GUREVICH:	Pearl of the Antilles. Queen of the Two Sicilies. Do you really have to sleep on this holey sofa?
NATALIE:	What can I do, Lev? If I've got night duty . . .

GUREVICH:	And you . . . and you sleep on this
	    mattress here!
	You, Natalie! You should be lifted off
	That mattress — you should be set to
	    music!

NATALIE:	You're beginning to chirr again, to chirr.

Coughing on the other side of the door again.

GUREVICH: "The majority of orthopteran males can chirr, whereas the females have lost this ability." *Textbook of General Entomology.*

They're drawn to each other again.

PROKHOROV: (*appears in the doorway with a mop and pail*) All the procedures— pro-ce-dures . . .

Exchanges looks with Gurevich. Prokhorov's look says, "Well, how did it go?" Gurevich's: "All square."

Natalia Alexeyevna, all expectations to the contrary, our new patient is getting stronger by the hour. But I just walked by, and your linoleum by the supply room door's gone all to hell—I can't stand it. But the newcomer . . . Well, just so he doesn't forget where he's landed, let him apply a little elbow grease there for half an hour. I'll supervise.

GUREVICH: Well, all right. (*Glancing at Natalie one last time, moving off with mop and pail, biting his lip strategically.*)

PROKHOROV: It's all above board. I'm your man. Alexeyevna, look after him. His head's fucked up. But that's okay.

Curtain.

ACT FOUR

Ward 3 again, but sparsely populated. Some aren't back from supper yet; others aren't back from their Aminazine shots. Kom-sorg Pashka Eryomin is still under the same sheet, in anticipation of the same tribunal. Old Man Khokhulya is immobilized after his electroshock, and no one's particularly concerned about whether he's breathing or not. Vitya is asleep, and so is the rear admiral. Stasik is struck dumb in the middle of the ward with his arm flung out in an SS salute. It's quiet. Only granddad Vova, the tip of his nose crimson, is talking.

VOVA:　　　　　　　Go on with you, it's glorious in the countryside right now! Come morning, as soon as you wake up, first thing, you take off your boots, the nice sun peeks into your eyes, but you can't look it in the eye. You're ashamed. You go out on the front steps, and the nightingale birdies gush: tweet tweet, cheep cheep, cuckoo, cock-a-doodle-doo, boc-boc-boc. Heaven on earth. You put on your jacket, take your ID, and go out in the steppe, naked as a jaybird, to shoot perch. You go wretched, barefoot, and hairy. But you

can't go without hair, thinking's easier
with hair, and when you go, you kiss all
the dandelions you meet on your way,
and the dandelions kiss your very faded,
unbuttoned shirt, which looks like it went
with you all the way from Berlin to Texas.

Seryozha Kleinmikhel and Kolya step into the ward very quietly,
holding hands. They're rubbing the shot sites on their butts, and
they sit down around Vova to listen.

And you walk on, and the winds blow
crosswise. Blue up above, emerald dew-
drops of May below. Up ahead, something dark shows up white. You wonder
whether it's just a hawthorn bush. But
no. An Armenian maybe? But no, where's
an Armenian going to come from in
the horsetails? Turns out, it's my grandson, Sergunchik. He's just four, he's only
started growing little hairs on his back —
but he can already tell everything apart,
every blade of grass from every other
blade of grass, and he studies every fledg-
ling by its innards.

KOLYA:
I can't tell things apart at all. I'm always
on the ward. I could still tell a plane
tree from a maple. But a maple from a
plane . . .

STASIK:
(*once again blows around the ward from*
corner to corner) Yes! There's nothing in
the world more important! Saving trees!
The occupier comes, and where's our
intimate defense? The intimate defense

of the educated partisan! What does it consist of? Just this: The educated partisan sits a bit and walks around, smokes a little and whistles. And horrifies the beautiful Klara!

VOVA: But my neighbor Nikolai Semyonovich —

STASIK: (*uncontrollably*) The Lord created light, yes, yes! And your Nikolai Semyonovich separated the light from the darkness. Now no one can tell the darkness from anything else. So they won't give us anything genuine and intimate! Boiled pearl barley, for example, with pot cheese, and raisins, and Hawaiian rum.

KOLYA: And vermouth.

STASIK: No, no vermouth. Why bring up vermouth? And how long are people going to keep interrupting me? Make the paths of the ungodly thorny? When, at last, will the creep toward nuclear disaster end? Why is the Divinity dawdling with retribution? And in general, when are those Poles going to quit bullshitting us? After all, life is short enough as is.

VOVA: Go plant a flower or something, Stas, and you'll feel better.

STASIK: Ho ho! Look who's giving who advice! Just take a gander at my greenhouse. Life's short, but when you look at my greenhouse, that life of yours is going to be even shorter! Your blades of grass

and buttercups—well, they're every-
where. But look what I have—I raised
this sort myself and watched it vegetat-
ing. It's called Pauncho-Blowup-Parasite,
with concave leaves, and boy, does it
bloom! Makes you want to fire a gun in
the air. It blooms so much, you feel like
shooting the first person to walk by! And
also, and also, if you want, Iron Bitch—
that's because once it starts blooming, it
goes around in its underwear! Comely
Pensive Hag is its best double variety.
Mama, I Can't Anymore; Sikhote-Alin;
and Phooey on You, Oh You. Yellow
Dumbbell! Whiner Tot! That's for anyone brought out feet first. Red Banner
Frump! Shaggy Chapaev! Fleeting Bull-
shitter! Whatever you want.

VOVA: You had all that in your garden, buddy?

STASIK: What do you mean, "had"? I still do!
                   What, Vova, you need them for your
                   knickers?

VOVA: I don't have knickers.

STASIK: Well, no, but you will, and naturally
                   you're going to want to trim your knickers
                   with something crimson at the top.
                   Come to my garden—and it's all yours.
                   Mincing Presumption, also known as
                   Luscious Palpated Zinochka—and how
                   could Zinochka not be palpated if she's
                   so luscious! Keen-Witted Scammers!
                   Socialist Inspector Darling! Chechen-
                   Ingush Gulf Stream! Half-Baked

Plenum!—called that for its smoke veils, incidentally, and definitely not to be witty. Twice-Decorated Modest Hegemon, and its best varieties: *Kappelmeister* Shtutsman, Ear-Nose-Throat, Rosemary-Never-Fade, and Kiss Me to Death. Bulb-Nosed General Secretary! And its purple varieties have all kinds of names: Love Can't Joke; Thunder of Victory, Ring Out; Cruiser Varangian; and Tits Awry. And if—

VOVA: Do you have blue ones? Me, when I go out in the field, through the dew, on major holidays, I look and look, and there aren't any blue ones.

STASIK: How can I not have blue ones! Imagine me not having blue ones! Look—spiritual nosies, smashed nosies, blue-curled *Guten Morgen* bibs! Dumbfucked Zanzibar—choose one: Losino Island, Yauza, Northerner, Silver Hoar, How-Do-You-Do, Leave Without Tears and For Good.

Stasik, at "Without Tears and For Good," freezes again by the ward window with his Rot Front fist flung up vertically.

VOVA: Y-yes, pretty flowers, but I remember hard times, you know, when all flowers vanished out of mind, good and bad alike. There was nothing around our village but escarpments and janissaries, trenches, helmets, arms, and legs—and only the tsar-cannons rumbled over Moscow, and the tsar-bells. But Army Gen-

eral Andrei Vlasov rose up, and after
him came Yuri Levitan, the announcer
on Soviet national radio—and together
they drove the legions of brutal overseas
hordes from the capital. And once again
the lungwort bloomed.

*Everyone is looking at Vova's nose. Kolya's nose is running again,
and Vova gently wipes it. Almost no one notices when the monitor
Prokhorov first invades and glances at his watch—he alone in the
entire ward has permission to wear a watch—and disappears once
again. The music throughout has been extremely disturbing.*

KOLYA: You know, it's nice in the countryside in
the fall, too. Isn't that right, Vova?

VOVA: Fall is a little worse: the ceiling drips.
You're sitting on the bare floor, and from
above, drip-drip, drip-drip, and the mice
are running across the floor, shur-mur,
shur-mur; sometimes you take pity on
one of them, grab it, and tuck it under
your arm to let it dry out and warm up.
There are two portraits on the opposite
wall, and I love them both, only I don't
know whose eyes are sadder: Lermontov
the hussar's or Comrade Pelshe's. Lermontov is so young, after all, he doesn't
understand anything, and he tells me,
"Vova, go to Cherepovets, and they'll
give you free boots." I say to him, "What
do I need boots for? Cherepovets is
so-o-o far away. If I get boots in Cherepovets, where am I supposed to go in
the boots from there? No, I'm better off
without the boots." And Comrade Pelshe

quietly says to me, to the sound of dripping water, "Might we be to blame for your sorrow, Vova?" And I say, "No, no one is to blame for my sorrow." Now there's a baby calf behind the partition — it's swearing and asking to start something — and I haven't fed it in ages, but where did it come from, this little calf? Because I've never had a cow. I need to ask my grandson Sergunchik — but the wind's whisked him off somewhere. The wind's whisked everyone off somewhere. Last evening I put a mug of buckwheat groats by the front steps — for the hedgehogs. When twilight fell, the mug started rattling, which meant the hedgehogs had come after all, to scrounge around. Leaves were circling in the air, circling and — landing on the bench. Some of them were lifted up again — and dropped back down on the bench. The flowers had all been transplanted for the winter. The wind kept driving the clouds, driving them north, northeast, north, and northwest. I didn't know which of them was coming back. While overhead, faster and faster, drip-drip-drip, and the wind was picking up. The trees began to creak and fail, crash and perish, without trial or investigation. Even the birds flew like heads off shoulders.

KOLYA: How nice. In our village — does April have thirty days, too, or have they tacked on a few extra?

VOVA:	Not yet.
KOLYA:	Well, that's too bad. They should add a few. Everything of ours should be bigger than theirs. They play a five-string guitar, and we have our own primordial seven-string. Baikal, the TV tower, the Caspian Lake. But it's a pity: they have thirty days in April, and so do we. (*Drools. Vova wipes it away.*) Pulling even with Europe, I think, which means lagging hopelessly behind it. Naturally, we aren't looking for one-sided advantages for ourselves, but we will never let—

Prokhorov bursts into the ward with a lit-up face.

| PROKHOROV: | Rounds! Rounds! (*But it's odd. Instead of the usual "Everyone up!" the monitor gives an order unlike any other.*) Lie down on the floor immediately! Everyone! Kissers down! Anyone shifts his eyes sideways, I'll fire every one of my LePage barrels! Stas, quit your Rot Fronts! |

Walks up to Stasik, but Stasik's arm catatonically won't relax out of its Rot Front state.

Oh, all right, just face the wall. *No pasarán! La Pasionaria! Venceremos!*

Gurevich enters with the mopping pail, a wet rag thrown over the top. Leaves the mop by the door. Approaching his nightstand, he hastily removes the rag, takes a bottle out of the pail that's nearly as big as the pail, and puts it away covered with the rag. Lets out a very deep breath.

GUREVICH:	There we are. Now it's like a victory!
ALYOKHA:	(*from the threshold*) Everyone, get up and shake yourself off! Rounds are over!
PROKHOROV:	Everyone, lie down on your bed. Notice, psychos, that rounds are getting shorter and shorter. That means they'll stop altogether before you know it. Up, up— and to your beds. Yes, yes. What were you doing here? While the leap-year people of our planet were achieving the impossible, what were you doing at the time, you lethargic nation?
VOVA:	Stasik was telling us about his nice flowers. He grows them himself.
PROKHOROV:	Well, lah-di-dah! Pretty flowers—they're inside us. You'll agree with me, Gurevich. Well, what are the pretty flowers on the outside worth?
GUREVICH:	You should skip me, Prokhorov. Later we can . . . There are lots of pretty flowers inside us anyway: cysts on our kidneys, cirrhoses in our liver, influenza and rheumatism from stem to stern, myocardia in the heart, abstinences from head to toe. Protuberances in the eyes.
PROKHOROV:	Pour sixty-five grams, Gurevich, and knock it back quick. We'll talk pretty flowers afterward. Alyokha!
ALYOKHA:	Here I am.

PROKHOROV:	Make it snappy: a glass of cold water. Khokhulya's got lemons in his suitcase—get them all out.
ALYOKHA:	All of them?
PROKHOROV:	All of them, damn your eyes!

Gurevich is essentially initiating Walpurgis Night. He pours a shot. Gives it a sniff, frowns hard, and gulps it down.

	(*in anticipation of his dose*) I used to think worse of you, Gurevich. I used to think worse of all of you. You tortured us in gas chambers, you rotted us on scaffolds. Turns out, nothing of the kind. Here's what I used to think: Better keep my distance from you! A distance big as a pogrom. But I see you're Alcibiades! Phooey, we're done with Alcibiades. You're Count Cagliostro! You're Canova, who sculpted Casanova, or the other way around—who cares! You're Lev! Isakovich, it's true, but still Lev! Gnaeus Pompeius and Marshal Mannerheim! Higher praises than these I've yet to find, but if I had sixty-five—
ALYOKHA:	Maybe we should check—does it burn?
GUREVICH:	That we can do. (*Pours a little of what's left on the edge of his nightstand, lights a match, and brings it close. Silence until the blue flame flickers.*)

Prokhorov doesn't even dilute his seventy grams; has a Khokhulya lemon at the ready. Tosses it back. Takes a passionate inhale of the lemon. A pause in self-absorption.

PROKHOROV: So. Humanity's starless hours are over!
              Tell me, Gurevich, what kind of marble
              should we cut you out of?

GUREVICH: What's this about cutting me out?

PROKHOROV: No, no. That's not what I meant. Here's
              what I meant. From this moment on, if
              in Ward 3 or any of our vassal wards some
              obtuse psycho doubts that this (*he pokes
              Gurevich*) nation is filled with the divine
              spirit, he will immediately be promoted
              by me to rear admiral. With all the ensu-
              ing consequences. They discover every-
              thing for the world; we barely manage to
              cover it up. What can you say about the
              Old World? Each and every one of us
              knows what tribe Christopher Colum-
              bus hailed from ultimately. But not
              many know that the first person from the
              Columbus expedition, the first to step on
              the New Land, was the Marano Jew Luis
              de Torres! (*Falling into a rage.*) And Isaac
              Newton! And Abraham Lincoln! And
              who was the first to see Niagara Falls?
              David Livingston!

GUREVICH: No rush, no rush, monitor. Or else you'll
              sow panic in weaker souls. Did you ever
              consider the fact that Alcibiades has long-
              ings, too? You're starting to go overboard
              on wearing the purple. Take a look at
              Alyokha.

PROKHOROV: Alyokha!

ALYOKHA: Here I am.

While Gurevich is doing his magic with alcohol and water, Al-yokha can't help himself. He makes a face. He strums his belly, as if accompanying himself on the guitar. Suddenly he starts an andante, too.

> In the whole wide world—I don't
>   care.
> I don't care if I smell like underwear,
> If the filthy wine I drink tastes bad
> Without the slightest thing to add.
> I'm happy to be degenerate,
> Happy my hooch is denaturate,
> So happy I can't remember where
> I heard the factory whistle blare.

He guzzles everything poured for him. Lets out a gigantic breath. Tries jauntily continuing his traditional:

> I've gotta,
> I've gotta,
> I've gotta make that redhead mine!
> Poom poom poom poom!

Over his own tum, naturally.

> I've gotta—

GUREVICH: Stop, Alyokha. I'm not up for canticles.
               The minor nations around us are thirsty.
               Meanwhile we, the superpowers, are
               tasting that which makes our souls au-
               tonomous, generally speaking, but could
               doom those same souls to something,
               too. Minister to these orphaned souls?

PROKHOROV: Minister and how! Alyokha!

ALYOKHA: Here I am.

Mechanically sets up an empty glass.

GUREVICH: Dimwit. Do you understand what
                   orphanhood is?

ALYOKHA: How could I not? Seryozha Klein-
                   mikhel — before his very eyes Pashka
                   Eryomin the Komsorg tore nearly every-
                   thing away from his mama. Now he's
                   forever scribbling and writing, scribbling
                   and writing. Call him over?

GUREVICH: Call him, call him.

Pours half a glass.

PROKHOROV: Kleinmikhel! On the carpet.

GUREVICH: *(to Seryozha, who is now nearby)* So what
                   did your mama wink to you about before
                   her death?

SERYOZHA: *(bursting into tears, of course)* She knew
                   everything. Mamas always know every-
                   thing. That I wouldn't be allowed to, and
                   the bosses wouldn't let me, make a film
                   about my mama and Semyon Mikhailo-
                   vich Budyonny and how hard they kissed
                   each other before the decisive battle. And
                   that Pashka Eryomin put his unclean
                   hand to it, the Jewish shpy.

GUREVICH: No rush. Drink up.

*Seryozha drinks up, then presses hand to heart as a sign of either
gratitude or seriously wishing to depart this world.*

SERYOZHA: I know what a Jewish shpy is. The first
                   sign is his name's Pashka. And his last's

	Eryomin. No other proof needed. At night he won't let me draw my poems and plans for the whole future.
GUREVICH:	What's that you're holding, Budyonny?
SERYOZHA:	It's what I'm hiding from the traitor Pashka. It's everything I'm going to build when they let me go. But if I do build anything, Pashka, the scoundrel, is going to set fire to it all. I'll read it to you now, but don't let Pashka Eryomin get close with his matches.
PROKHOROV:	Here, let me read it, you bore. Because I have a baritone and you don't. Yes, yes. Plan for future rejoicing. Number one: A hospital for smashed-up cosmonauts. Number two: A house of love and health for sick cosmonauts. Number three: A house of Love for my mama, as good and nice as possible. Number four: A house where people don't party until twelve o'clock at night and live with their near and dear sometimes and in general. Number five: A House of Communism, where they teach you not to run with an ax and not to drink away children and cosmonauts. Number six: A Cultivated Stadium for Cosmonauts, to throw them at a target.
GUREVICH:	Is this bore going to drag on much longer? Quit letting Seryozha—
PROKHOROV:	Just a minute, just a minute. (*Continues.*) Number seven: A Book Factory for Culti-

vated Pilots, with hypno-sedative effects. Number eight: A House and a Cultivated Road for Athletic Tatars. Number nine: An Airport of Culture for Tatars and Cosmonauts. Ten: A Train Station for Trains. So girls in short skirts can stand on the steps and wave to the arriving and departing trains.

Alyokha snorts.

(*continues*) An Attentive Athletics Institute. An Attentive Athletics Traffic Light for Tatars and Cosmonauts. An Attentive Athletics Cosmic School for All Airports of the Cosmos. Number fourteen and penultimate: A Children's World on an athletics river. Where little spies drown and big ones float to the surface to give important and false testimony. Number fifteen and last: A Cosmic Exhibit of the Cheerful Love and Secret Joys of All the Cheerful Cosmonauts of the Cheerful Cosmos.

GUREVICH: Mmm, yes. Maybe Komsorg Eryomin was right in dismembering your mama?

SERYOZHA: No, he was deeply wrong. When she was whole, she was much more adornful. You can have your laugh, but there's really no call for laughing. I have one other project, for there to be less laughter in Russia: a pipeline from Frankfurt am Main, via Urengoy, Pomary, and Uzhgorod, to Smolensk and Novopolotsk.

	A pipeline to supply tear gas to Russia. On mutually advantageous terms.
GUREVICH:	Bravo, Kleinmikhel! Monitor, pour him a little more.

The monitor pours. Patting Seryozha on the head, he serves him. Seryozha, touched by the praise, downs a quick one and grunts.

SERYOZHA:	I also like it when Lyudmila Zykina sings. When she sings, everything about me bursts, even the socks I just bought— those burst, too. Even my shirt under my arms—it bursts. My nose runs, my tears run, and everything about the Home- land, about the flowering of our bound- less fields.
GUREVICH:	Wonderful, Serzh, console yourself that at least your accursed enemy, the Kom- sorg, isn't going to get a single gram. Un- fortunately, he is part of the nation's total headcount. A moron with a serious form of frivolity, chockablock voids. He has no twilights, no dawns, not even full-fledged bastardy. In my opinion, it'd be better to give full amnesty to prisoners of con- science. I mean, after a preliminary slap. Untie the rear admiral?
PROKHOROV:	Well, naturally. Especially since he woke up a long time ago, the Pentagon's nuclear hostage.

Wipes his hands, pours another for Gurevich, himself, and Alyokha.

Up, commander. NATO's unsinkable air-
craft carrier. I'm going to untie you now.
'Fess up, Nelson: Isn't it nice living in the
world of supreme justice?

Little by little they free Mikhalych from his fetters.

MIKHALYCH: I need a drink.

PROKHOROV: This man is totally one of us! But first
                        kneel and say your final word.

Mikhalych shudders.

                        No, just make your apologies to the great
                        insulted nation, and so your former
                        friends and acquaintances from the
                        North Atlantic pact can hear you. Oh,
                        I don't know, some prayer.

MIKHALYCH: (*very quickly, glancing at Prokhorov,
                        who is pouring for him in advance*)
                                Moscow's such a clever town: belly
                                        up and slam one down.
                                A sick man's Lent, a sober one's
                                        prayer; God doesn't hear them
                                        anywhere.
                                Tea and coffee go against my grain.
                                        A morning vodka suits my brain.
                                Glass one's a shock, glass two's a
                                        hawk, and the rest are little birdies.
                                Drink is trouble; not drinking's
                                        double. Drink too little and end
                                        up rubble.
                                Just looking at beer always fills me
                                        with cheer.

PROKHOROV: (*much livelier than in Act 2*) Yes, yes, yes.

MIKHALYCH: Don't water, and the cabbage dries
                                        out. Where'd I get this freezing
                                        snout?
                              Time to pour one down the spout.
                              Germans to my right; to my left,
                                        Turks. Oh, fuck this jive; they're
                                        all jerks.
                              Feels colder now. Must be time—

GUREVICH: It is time, my friend, it is.

*The admiral drinks up and goggles at the strength of the drink
and the change in his earthly lot.*

                              According to our Constitution, admiral,
                              every citizen has the right to goggle, but
                              not that hard. Vova!

*Vova comes to him meekly but is holding pale Kolya's hand for
some reason.*

                              Children, the Armenian brandy's on the
                              table. Say a prayer. (*To Prokhorov.*) And
                              just why are they here—and not there?

PROKHOROV: Well, you heard yourself. The Estonian
                              has a headache. Isn't that enough? As
                              for Vova, he's just like that. Suspected of
                              being unique.

GUREVICH: Don't grieve, Vova. Tomorrow you and I
                              will be free. Do you have a dream?

VOVA: Yes, yes, I do. I want to raise a certain
                              kind of fish at home, in a pond; it's called
                              a gambusia. So you see, this fish, the

	gambusia, it'll eat up all the mosquito eggs in my pond, and all the lamblias at the same time. Because all you have to do is swallow one lamblia in your water, and it gives birth to another lamblia all by itself, and to a third lamblia born of the combining of the first two lamblias.
GUREVICH:	And how many of these lamblias of yours can your gambusia fish swallow at once?
VOVA:	It can pack away seventy-five at one go.
GUREVICH:	And not choke?
VOVA:	And not choke.
GUREVICH:	Excellent. Now pour him exactly that many grams. Only dilute it with water. Tonight Borenka the Goon is going to pay for that "modus vivendi" he put on your nose.

Vova, finishing it off in a single gulp, first turns green as grass, then bright as the sun.

VOVA:	Most of all, what's good about the gambusia is that it means there's not a single mosquito in the air. No one bites you. You go boldly into the forest, my young radio listeners. And walk around until Edik calls for you.
PROKHOROV:	Who is this Edik?
VOVA:	No one knows. But as soon as Hesperus rises in the heavens, you have to disperse to your houses because Edik gives the

signal that it's time. There's nothing you can do. Sergunchik, my grandson, didn't listen—and the result? The winds carried him off somewhere, on order of State TV and Radio.

GUREVICH: Russia really is an amazing country! So how does Edik fit in? What's Edik's excuse? (*To Kolya.*) Kolya! Can you make sense of this hodgepodge?

KOLYA: Of course. I mastered that dharma long ago. (*Reaching out to his audience.*) Our fathers ate sour grapes, yet our children's table has only vermouth, nothing else. Sluiced with sweet vermouth, Onegin hastens to the youth, looks at him, and calls to him—in vain. The young singer's met a ghastly end. A special vodka he demanded, living torment filled his gaze— and to him someone handed sweet vermouth—sideways!

GUREVICH: Great! Pour the poet some mushcatel!

KOLYA: (*drinking his share of muscatel*) Where did our ward ever get mushcatel?

PROKHOROV: It's all from there. Where did our ward get curious youths with their imbecilic questions? If we got it, we got it. Meanwhile, we've lost nothing but our honor. If more questions come up, ask Vitya.

GUREVICH: Yes, yes. If something's not clear, let them go to our unforgettable grandmaster. What an honor, to be called unforget-

table in one's lifetime! Vi-tya! Korchnoi!
What's new, schizoo?

*Everyone looks at Vitya. It's not entirely clear whether he's asleep
or awake, because his smile, which remains on duty while he's
asleep, becomes sardonic upon awakening. Right now there's no
trace of that.*

	Well, it's very easy to tell whether some-one's asleep or not. If he wants to join the party, that means he woke up. If he doesn't, he must be asleep and never is going to wake up.
VITYA:	I'm awake. As long as the world doesn't run out of mushcatel, I'll never fall asleep.
PROKHOROV:	(*serving Vitya*) Now do you understand, grandmaster, that we live not in the world of supreme justice but in a world of the kind of justice that's actually even higher than the highest?
VITYA:	(*lifting his large, pink head*) I'm not going to die?
GUREVICH:	You hold too high an opinion of yourself, Vitya. In the entire drama so far—until you came along—no one has uttered a word about death, though everyone has bent an elbow. Man's happiness lies in himself, in the satisfaction of natural human demands. Pierre Bezukhov. If death comes, so be it. Death is just one nasty moment, not worth taking seri-ously. Augusto Sandino.

Vitya drinks and—gets up. Taking in everyone with his smile—and not embarrassed by his belly—he heads for the exit for some reason.

PROKHOROV: At last! The delight and horror of the Universe—Vitya—decides to take a stroll in the direction of the toilet. Stasik! Quit your Rot Fronts! Come over here.

GUREVICH: (*suddenly remembering*) Yes, yes. There'll be no more Rot Fronts or *No pasárans* now. There are clear skies over all Hishpania. Francisco Franco. That said, lower your foolish arm and come closer. Your furious Dolores is in the next department. Down 120 for courage, and we'll unite you, you halfwits.

STASIK: You mean she isn't dead yet?

GUREVICH: She croaked a long time ago. But as soon as she heard about you and your impending tryst, she shook the earth from her eye sockets and said, "Have him come see me. I love the young and corrupt. But first," she said, "but first I have to get myself in shape. After all, I've been lying in the damp earth for so long."

STASIK: I understand. A woman is always a woman, even if she's La Pasionaria. We have things to talk about: the massive pressure on Islamabad, the submarines in the steppes of Ukraine! And on top of everything else, the rapist Uncle Vasya in the dill thickets. And the puppet Chun

	Doo-hwan, he keeps dreaming of wiping Soviet Russia off the face of the earth. But can you really wipe off something that has so very much land — and no face whatsoever? That's what the slant eyes of those Chun Doo-hwans lead to.
GUREVICH:	Pour him one immediately! In proportion to what he's expostulated here now. My God, Vitya!
VITYA:	(*with a smile more captivating than any since the Creation*) Here, please, is a chess piece, I washed it in running water.

Places yet another white queen on the table in the middle of the ward. Two white queens side by side — it's too much. Many are losing what's left of their miserable reason.

| PROKHOROV: | We'll sort out the chess afterward. But the checkers — where are they? World champion in Russian checkers Viktor Kuperman. [Jewish] (*A smile directed at Gurevich, the question addressed to Vitya.*) There you have it. No checkers. Now our Russian comrade Kuperman looks at the world distraughtly. Here he is, young and healthy, spinning in his grave. Don't confuse him with Dolores Ibárruri. He's spinning in his grave, even though he's young and healthy. |
| KOLYA: | (*interrupts the monitor, something that's never happened to the monitor before*) Who in fact is the author of the gastro-intestinal tract? |

GUREVICH: Do you really not understand who by
                      now?

Sits down beside Vitya.

                              Just tell me, Vitya, you know,
                                  what if you . . .
                              Well, if twenty-six Baku
                                  commissars . . .
                              That's outrageous! If so, what
                                  would you
                              Bring the crowd from the bottom
                                  of your heart?
                              Shpinoza? An SS *Gruppenführer?*
                              A smashing finish to a jubilee?
                              René Descartes?

*Heels heard outside the door. It's Natalie on her last rounds.
Thank God, she's already a little May Day tipsy. Otherwise, she
would have picked up on the alcohol in the ward.*

PROKHOROV: Quiet! Everyone to their places! Heads
                      under the covers!

*Natalie comes in and wishes everyone goodnight. Straightens
the blankets that need straightening. Sits down at the head of Gurevich's bed. Whispering and tender words that no one — or maybe
everyone — can hear.*

NATALIE: (*in a half-whisper*) Don't worry about a
                      thing, Lev. It's all going to be fine.

*Gurevich tries to say something. Natalie presses her finger to
his lips.*

                              Shh. Everyone's dozing. Not a soul in the
                              hallway. Adieu. Goodnight, alkies.

Natalie sails toward the exit and closes the door very softly behind her. *The rap of retreating heels.*

All the patients throw off their blankets at once, sit up in their beds, and gaze, bewitched, at the two white queens in the middle of the ward.

Curtain.

ACT FIVE

Between Acts 4 and 5, five to seven minutes of music like nothing else and anything at all: a mix of Georgian lezginkas, turn-of-the-century café-chantant dances, the silly intro to Varlaam's part in Mussorgsky's opera, cancans and cakewalks, slapstick Russian dances, and the most bravura motifs taken from Magyar operettas from the era of the Austro-Hungarian monarchy's fall.

The curtain rises.

The same Ward 3, a few hours later. Everyone looks so different, even mentioning it is ridiculous.

PROKHOROV: Getting light! Alyokha!

ALYOKHA: Yes, here I am.

PROKHOROV: Smack something on your guitar, Dissident! Smack the hearts of our enlightened prisoners!

ALYOKHA: Poom poom poom poom.

The performance begins. Everyone joins in, even Komsorg Pashka Eryomin. What hole he crawled out of no one knows. After all, he'd been refused a single gram.

> Poom poom poom poom!
> Poom poom poom poom!

Spanish and Portuguese Club

Upcoming Events:

Conversation Tables
Hagerty Cafe, 3pm-5pm, ~~Mondays~~

Día de Los Muertos Celebration
November 3rd, 6:00pm- 8:00pm
Enarson Classroom Bldg 202
Come for traditional Mexican snacks, crafts, and Spanish music!

Study Abroad Panel
November 13th, 5:30-7:00pm
Maudine Cow Room, Ohio Union
We will have several students talk about their experiences abroad and answer any questions you may have, as well as an advisor from OIA.

Talk with Evan Davis
November 17th, 11am-12
Lower level Meeting Room, Ohio Union
A personal conversation with Evan Davis, an accomplished Ohio State Alum. He was very involved with the International Affairs Department, won the Thomas Pickering Fellowship, and is about to go to Rio as a Foreign Service Officer. Get ideas about how to pursue a career path in foreign language!

To be added to our email list: send an email to grin.stead.11

President: Lizzie Pilsner (pilsner.3)
Vice President (and community service): Kathryn Gasior (gasior.12)
Treasurer (and conversation tables): Michelle Meek (meek.81)
Webmaster: Leron Robinson (leronr@earthlink.net)

Consecration of Spring
Alejo Carpenté

Nora Zúñiga — Show
(dance department)

Laura Podalski
(urban film)
Theater department

I'll put on a dress of white
And add a coat of spring.
I'm not afraid of anything:
The chairman is my father.

VOVA: The chairman rushes in to see us.
He says, "This isn't grievous."
He tells us not to sentimentalize.
His advice instead: "Go fertilize."

MIKHALYCH: The children waded through their
    morning slog,
Washed, and shaved, and the hair of
    the dog.
Oh, for the love of God the father,
Give us a smoke!

KOLYA: He's twenty already,
But he's a proper fool!
He's thirty already,
But he's a proper fool!
He's forty already,
But he's a proper fool!
He's—

ALYOKHA: (*interrupts him*) Kolya thinks that
    he's a pilot—
And this is very good
Vova gobbles all his compote—
This is also very good!

PROKHOROV: But the spy from Minnesota
Is very good as well.

    This, naturally, is a jab at Mikhalych, who that very moment is attempting some hocus-pocus with his hands, like Saint-Saëns' Plisetskaya swan.

This spy of beauty unsurpassed
Spilled the red wine from her glass,
Spilled it on her satin breast
And slept the sleep of the perfectly
    blest.
Ho ho!

ALYOKHA:

Poom poom poom poom!
The whole country lies in gloom
A light is burning in the Kremlin!
Poom!
I adore that tender hokum
When it's near the perineum!

Vitya and his belly break into a dance; he ties on a pillowcase instead of a scarf.

(*dances up to Vitya*)

Hey-hey! Oh-ho!
It's all set. Bobik croaked.
Manechka, what's wrong with you?

VITYA:

(*not without flirtation*)

Absolutely nothing,
No more than nothing.
Nothing happened to Manechka.
She just twirled too much.
She just wanted so much
To go in a year or two
To Pisa or to Kathmandu!
Oh yeah!

PROKHOROV:

Curls curl,
Curls curl,
Whores have curls that curl.
Why don't curls ever curl
On the decent people of the world?

VITYA:	Hee! Hee! The reason they don't curl Is those people don't have the cash for curls!
ALYOKHA:	(*correcting Vitya*) Because it's only whores Who have curler cash, And decent people Just have cash for ass.

Gurevich is meanwhile worriedly examining the half-drowsy Khokhulya, who is clearly about to keel over, having drunk every drop of his 115 grams. Gurevich walks over and shakes him.

GUREVICH:	Khokhulya! Want to knock some more back to revive your psyche? Can you hear me? He can't. I'll give it to you letter by letter, Khokhulya. Drink—*dyornut*—"d" for the disaligned movement, Dwight Eisenhower, dainty dreams, divine hips, the Day of the Dead. "D." Next, "yo." Only how can I convey "yo" to him? That scoundrel Karamzin. He came up with "zh" but no "yo." After all, Cyril and Methodius already had "b" and "kh" and "zh." But no, that wasn't enough for that aesthete Karamzin. Stop, boys! Khokhulya isn't breathing! died!

Some of them come to stand around the dead man; others continue their feckless rampage.

PROKHOROV:	That's what electroshock leads to! Here you have brilliant confirmation of the bankruptcy of our medicine!

Stasik stands by the corpse like a guard at Lenin's Tomb, his jaw jutting out.

GUREVICH:
It's all right. No surprise. We should put all our trust in fate and firmly believe that the worst is yet to come.

PROKHOROV:
(*adds*) René Descartes. And no one is going to be gloomy! Today we're celebrating the Walpurgian festival of strength, beauty, and grace! Let ordinary people celebrate May Day—that is, not ordinary people but the staff that serve us! Ha ha! Everybody, dance! Ladies' choice! Alyokha!

ALYOKHA:
Poom poom poom poom!
Poom poom poom poom!
I do love everything,
I do love everything:
Detective stories,
British lorries,
Hawaiian guitars,
Havana cigars,
Wise men of Zion,
And twins of Siam.
Ooh ooh ooh ooh!

Set to a Tchaikovsky motif.

Go not to nibble,
Go not to fiddle,
Go not, I beg, to jiggle
Our maidenly calves.

VITYA:
(*in imitation of Kálmán, playing his tum*)

For what, my God, for what?

	For what, my God, for what?
	For what, my God, for what?
	For what, my God, for what?
KOLYA:	(*in imitation of a Soviet children's song*)

Yes, I have no vodkie,
Not even a vermouthie.

PROKHOROV: (*joins in*)

Only beer, only water!
Only water, only beer!
And not one of us is drunk!
Pour, pour, you madcaps.
Pour the stupefying stuff
Into the ceremonial glass!
Piff paff!

Approaches the flask of alcohol, pours, and tosses it back. The others would like to do the same, but Gurevich stops them.

GUREVICH: A little later. Kleinmikhel, come over here. I have good news for you. Your mama didn't die! She's alive. Pashka didn't kill her!

Pours for him.

SERYOZHA: (*pressing the filled glass to his heart*) Hurrah! My mama's alive!

PASHKA: Hurrah! I didn't kill her!

Instantly snatches the mug from Seryozha's hands and downs it in one gulp.

GUREVICH: You're crafty, Pasha, the way I see it. But I won't let you spoil the applause here.

> They'll bash you in the kisser—that's
> > for sure:
> "Privately, in a particular form."

PROKHOROV: René Descartes? (*To Pasha.*)

> In short, my gracious friend,
> Go for that pussy in the morning
> > dew!

Pasha, receiving a slap from the monitor and hiccupping, joins the dancers.

GUREVICH: No, just look, monitor, look at this playful and nauseating thing here. That means none of it, none of it, was in vain, all the revolutions, the religious strife, the dynasties' rise and fall, the Crucifixion and the Resurrection, the Bartholomew nights and the Volochaev days—all this, ultimately, just so Komsorg Eryomin could dance the kazachok for all he's worth. No, something's not right. Come here, Seryozha. I'll pour you a tad more.

Seryozha crosses himself and drinks up.

> Well, how are your cheerful cosmonauts of the Cosmos getting along?

SERYOZHA: (*animated by his five swallows,
dances in time with the others*)
> Cosmonauts and Tatars,
> Cosmonauts and Tatars,
> It's all a lie. It's shit, I say.
> They'll have to do it anyway.
> Come and take the guitars away.
> Hey!

GUREVICH: That's the way. And Vova? Where's Vova?
            What's with Vova?

Vova is sitting in bed, his head resting on the windowsill, not moving, and for some reason his mouth is wide open.

            Go take a look, Prokhorov. What's with
            him?

PROKHOROV: He's breathing! Vovochka's breathing!
            (*Sings him some Grieg.*) "Let us go into
            the forest, my dear friend, where the vio-
            lets await. Let us go into the forest, the
            forest green, where the violets await."

Vova doesn't respond with a single sound. His mouth is still open, but he's already met his Maker.

GUREVICH: But! There (*nods toward where the medi-
            cal staff's May Day party is under way*)
            they're having fun completely differ-
            ently. Oh, all right. We've been lost and
            still aren't found. But gossip surrounds
            them and legends surround us. We're
            plays; they're documentaries. They're de-
            limited, while we're unlimited. They're
            worldly-wise. We're just out of this world.
            They're barking; we're blazing. They have
            urges—

PROKHOROV: And we have surges. Stands to reason.
            You speak the truth! Their life's the pits,
            and ours is the cat's pajamas! We really
            know how to sing! They've got those Ro-
            tarus and Kobzons or some such. I would
            drown that beautiful Sofia Rotaru, only I
            don't know where's better, in shit or down

[handwritten marginal note: be ne fits of madness]

an ice hole. And I'd sell wonderful Iosif
Kobzon to Egypt for a fifth. Ho ho! That's
all there's to it!

*Takes tiny separate sips. The others lick their lips languidly on the
sidelines.*

It's about time Russia got radically started
on radical change! I've already renamed
the streets and drowned the stage singers.
You'd think the time had come.

GUREVICH: Yes, yes. The time should have come
to change those labels. Or else—well,
how insipid can you get? Jubilee Street,
Archer Street, Capital Street. When I see
that, it makes me sick. Vodka should be
like a tear, and all its subspecies should
be named tearfully. Like this, for instance: Flammable Maiden, 5 rubles
20 kopeks; Stingy Male, 7 rubles; Tur-
bid Stray, 4.20; Inconsolable Widow—
not too expensive either: 4.40; Bitter
Orphan, 6 rubles; Import Crocodile, a
tenner. Well, you get the idea. Only before smashing Russia in front of an aston-
ished humanity, first she needs to be enlightened.

PROKHOROV: Oh ho! Enlightened. Our neglect in all
spheres of knowledge—it's scary to think
about. For instance, I've asked quite a
few people how many cuts there really
are in a cut-glass glass. After all, each
Soviet glass has an identical number of
facets. And imagine: no one knows. Of

	145 people surveyed, only one answered correctly, and that was by accident. Before it's too late, I wonder, why not start an era of Enlightenment in Russia?
GUREVICH:	We already have. Within the confines of the third ward for now. Just look. Well, what was the Russian nation before us? Sluggish demonism, dismal extravagance. A recklessness woven of yawns. There was no honor, no excellence, no majesty at all. To say nothing of highness, let alone supremacy. When I was at liberty and gazed upon our Russians, sometimes I would be so flooded with sorrow I could barely squeeze onto a bus.
PROKHOROV:	(*pathetically*) Me too. I believe we're slightly underdone and underripe. But we do have an enchantment about us. I can tell from myself, and especially tonight.
GUREVICH:	It's all right, it's all right. We'll inform, deform, and deliver. And if anyone is still suffering from being only semi-strangled and half-slashed, then that, too, can be easily remedied.

Meanwhile, Alyokha, Vitya, Kolya, Seryozha, and Mikhalych have been slowly stealing up on the two thinkers and watching them with various degrees of adoration.

PROKHOROV:	Alyokha!
ALYOKHA:	Here we all are.

PROKHOROV:	Good that it's all of you.
GUREVICH:	Yes, exactly. In the stinking West, all any-one there does is stand in line for free soup. They get given soup by the Vati-can, or someone else—I don't know. But when they're doing it, they look to Russia and think—what they're thinking I don't know either. However, be that as it may, we must be ever on the alert and prepar-ing ourselves for great deeds! You, are you preparing yourself for a great deed?
VITYA:	Are we ever!
GUREVICH:	Well, that's just great.

He serves drinks to everyone in turn. Continues speaking mean-while.

	As a matter of fact, I feel sorry for them. Right now you and I hobnob in line—not for some pathetic Vatican soup but for something top-notch! That, too, must be remembered! And then, they're isolated: each has his own worry, his own rum-bling in the belly. Whereas we share our worry and our rumbling!
ALYOKHA:	Hurrah!
PROKHOROV:	Fool! Why the hell did you shout "Hur-rah"?
ALYOKHA:	Because they're isolated, and we're going to smother them like kittens!
PROKHOROV:	What do you think, Gurevich? Will we?

GUREVICH: Why smother them now? Why not
                   just—smother them! Of all the na-
                   tions, none is more peace-loving than
                   ours. But if they're going to have fur-
                   ther doubts about that, before too long
                   they'll surely pay for their mistrust of
                   our love for peace. Those sharks don't
                   care about anything but themselves.
                   Look, here's a Mozart lullaby: "Sleep, my
                   joy, go to sleep. Someone sighed in the
                   next room—what do we care, dear one?
                   Quickly, shut your little eyes." And so.
                   Forth. They—the Fritzes, that is—they
                   don't give a damn about anyone else's
                   misfortune, not the slightest sympathy for
                   anyone else's sigh. "Sleep, my joy." No,
                   we're not like that. Another person's mis-
                   fortune is our misfortune, too. We give
                   a damn about every sigh, and we have
                   no time to sleep. We've already reached
                   the point of such vigilance and authority
                   that we can take away not just someone's
                   sigh, a heavy sigh in the next room, but
                   their very inhaling and exhaling. As if we
                   would shut our eyes!

PROKHOROV: As I understand it, then, we should
                   smother them. I just don't know where
                   to start. With the Fritzes, no doubt.

GUREVICH: Give me a break, Prokhorov! What
                   Fritzes? For a Fritz not to breathe, we
                   wouldn't even have to swing our left leg.
                   A Fritz is barely breathing as it is!

VITYA: I'd punish the Dutch, for flying.

MIKHALYCH:	Then the Jews, for never dying.
PROKHOROV:	Shh! Gurevich, I suggest we take away the admiral's next round and demote him to cabin boy at the same time. For vulgarity.
GUREVICH:	If that's what you want, that's what we'll do.
ALYOKHA:	Personally, I'm interested in the British Isles.
GUREVICH:	Well, there's no point in pandering to Britain. Even Herodotus didn't believe in its existence. Why should we be any better or worse than Herodotus? Everyone has to be thoroughly convinced that it does not in fact exist, but we barely have to lift a finger for that.
PROKHOROV:	Let the Yanks quake a little in the meantime. I hope they have rotten, sleepless nights; no point in any good-byes to them.
KOLYA:	But look, if they tell me to smother Scandinavians, why should I? They're all very, very blond, too, and as innocent as the day is long.
GUREVICH:	You're wrong, Kolya. They need to be raked over the coals—for starters, for considering their stinking Vikings and Konungs the forefathers of our grand dukes. And later—for Quisling and for being seafarers in general.

PROKHOROV: (*joins in*) And for roaming freely to
                 both of our primordially Russian poles.
                 They're sons of bitches, not seafarers.
                 Bump them off! That's what I think.

MIKHALYCH: May we meet again soon, comrade
                 sailors! Give Nastenka your beret. That's
                 all.

*Collapses at the side of his bed like a bird shot down in flight and
starts snoring for all eternity.*

GUREVICH: What's with him? Is he joking? Or . . . ?

PROKHOROV: The cabin boy was just a little rocked by
                 our storms. It's nothing. The Italians, for
                 instance — we don't need him to deal
                 with them. A more vapid tribe the Lord
                 has not created since the beginning.
                 They're always wanting to hug, and that's
                 all they have. Just take those, oh, Sacco
                 and Vanzetti. Hugging. Well, let them
                 hug. Sacco is wonderful, body and soul.
                 Vanzetti never had a trace of soul, but
                 what shapes! Front and back both! But
                 shapes are shapes. Why toss our party
                 comrade Giordano Bruno on the camp-
                 fire like charcoal? If I were an Italian,
                 how could I dare to look into Russian
                 eyes after that!

ALYOKHA: Ugh, you've got me all worked up over
                 the wonderful Vanzetti's shapes! Give me
                 a nice Polish girl!

PROKHOROV: There aren't going to be any Polish girls!

VITYA:	Why not? Because of Taras Bulba? *what?*
GUREVICH:	I spit on your Bulba! Because they over-took us in geographical proximity to Europe, and—
PROKHOROV:	And in their historical hatred for the Jews.
ALYOKHA:	(*in imitation of his patron*) I have a pro-posal. Demote comrade Prokhorov to being my orderly, for vulgarity, and take away his next shot.
GUREVICH:	Now, that's going overboard! This joker just needs a little roughing up.

Prokhorov walks up to Alyokha and gives him a little quiet rough-ing up.

	Lord! They've got it all mixed up again! Oh, all right. Why don't you tell me, those of you prepared for great deeds, which of you likes the Frenchies?
EVERYONE:	Everyone!
GUREVICH:	(*sarcastically*) Everyone?
EVERYONE:	(*thinking better of it*) No one!
GUREVICH:	All right. What we have here is a plethora of crime: Bagration's right side, Alexan-der Pushkin's belly, Kutuzov's left eye, and—
KOLYA:	(*a little tipsy*) But that's the Turks! Kutu-zov's eye . . .

PROKHOROV:	What do the Turks have to do with this? What Turks? Our Bulgarian comrade Antonov shot all the Turks long ago with his rifle, on Saint Peter's Square in Rome. And I personally saw a fine painting of Kutuzov, and he was riding in on a horse, I don't remember where, but he had two eyes.
GUREVICH:	That's the whole point. A Russian shouldn't be one-eyed. These here— they can allow themselves this luxury, all these Admiral Nelson-Rockefellers. But not us; we can't. The Universe's alarming situation obliges us to keep both eyes open. Yes.

Applause.

KOLYA:	Lisbon, however, our Lisbon, so very beautiful!
PROKHOROV:	Where does Lisbon come into this? What is Lisbon anyway? Sluice it with water on all sides and don't let anyone out! That's the way. Or light fires on all sides of it and don't let anyone out!
GUREVICH:	The mere sound of the word "Lisbon" repulses me now. I'm flooded with bile when people say "Lisbon" in front of me. Should bile really flood a person? No, it shouldn't. That means there shouldn't be a Lisbon either!

Applause.

Kolya, do you need Lisbon?

KOLYA: Nah.

GUREVICH: What about you, Vitya?

VITYA: Not at all.

GUREVICH: There, you see? There are things in this world that absolutely no one needs—they bloom, they smell sweet, and they exist. While man still lacks what is most essential. In short, there will be no Lisbon. At the same time, though, can I count on my strategic allies?

ok…lo)

EVERYONE: (*higgledy-piggledy*) You can, Gurevich, you can! Let's have another quick swig!

GUREVICH: In the nick of time!

They each take a quick swig.

SERYOZHA: Good afternoon. Maybe it's evening. I can't know, of course. I hasten to send you greetings from a pure heart. Hello, dear departed mama, with greetings for you, from your son Fedya.

All of a sudden he starts laughing—which is unusual. After all, no one has even see him smile. He laughs, circles like a wolf cub, falls to the floor, and writhes in strange paroxysms.
Everyone is struck dumb briefly. Music.

GUREVICH: (*frowning*) Well, all right. His mama turned out to be alive—and he ended up dead as a result. There have been

instances in history of death from unexpected good news. Michel Montaigne.

*Stasik drops his mausoleum sentry pose and again starts pulsing
from corner to corner of the ward.*

STASIK: Those born under the Mark of Quality
                           can't remember their own path. But we,
                           the dregs of humanity, can't forget it!
                           Relax, people; shake your wrists. And
                           please, don't kill each other. That grieves
                           me. God is wiser than man! Cling to
                           Christ's raiment!

Turns to stone again, this time in a prayerful pose on bended knee.

GUREVICH: (*continues, full of inspiration*) But if there
                           is no Lisbon, obviously the other conti-
                           nents come crashing down of their own
                           accord. Starting with the Asiatic East.
                           That pernicious and sinister accumu-
                           lation of sewage has no right to exist!
                           Here's the Eastern inscription on the
                           stone, the tombstone—and that's from
                           Gospel times! "The universal favorite,
                           full of charm. Without mercy, he exter-
                           minated every last man."

Laughter in the room.

                           Well, what would you have us do with
                           those nations? Don't do anything!
                           They'll cash in their chips themselves.
                           They keep being racked by population
                           booms, furuncles, Hiroshimas, napalms,
                           and Nagasakis, and they've run out of
                           food. They'll die out quietly, all by them-

selves — and purge the earth and skies!
All the rest will be delivered by tick-borne
encephalitis, squabbles among Marxist
dictatorships, and the Manchurian fever.
The time for Retribution fast approaches!
Let's drink a drop, dear brethren, to the
time at hand!

ALYOKHA: I, for one, am in favor of the Manchurian
                   fever!

Drinks first, grunts, and tries to revive his presentation.

Poom poom poom poom.
Poom poom poom poom.
The apocalypse is today!
Rise up in your negligée,
Rise up, jump up: no more light.
No more right.
No more money.
Nothing holy.
Reagan's in Stromboli!

CHORUS: (*having already drunk and grunted*)
                   Everything down the hole,
                   Reagan's now in Oryol.

PROKHOROV: (*stentorianly*) This day of victory!

CHORUS: Prokhor is putrid!
                   This joy makes us wretched!
                   Our happiness insipid!
                   Victory Day!

GUREVICH: Shush! You drunken numbskulls! I see
                   you haven't understood any of my in-
                   spired insights! You've got it all mixed up.

PROKHOROV:	We all understood you perfectly, Gurevich. Only you forgot the fact that there's a U.N. and Pérez de Cuéllar. When the continents come crashing down—
GUREVICH:	Ha! Pérez de Cuéllar, naturally, is going to clutch his Peruvian head. Have you ever seen people with Peruvian heads? Here he is with his Peruvian head, and he goes and clutches it. Well, let him. All the same, no one's going to save the plague-infested world for us, you know! All of you, when you feast, don't forget the plague! Feasts are fine, but some things are more important than feasts. General Haig. Believe in the final Russian triumph inasmuch as they have the cross by their side and that's it. We have all the rest!

A sound that is incomprehensible at first. As if someone had bolted the door behind him with great force. Everyone turns around. It's Vova. And this is Vova's mouth, which has been open throughout Act 5, shutting forever. At nearly the same time the snores of Komsorg Eryomin under his sheet break off. Backstage "The Ancient Linden" plays.

Kolya, staggering, walks up to Vova and presses his ear to his heart.

| KOLYA: | Vova! Uncle Vova! Where are you going? Don't go. It's really nice in the forest now! And the scent is so fragrant. (*Cries like a baby.*) There are gambusias splashing in the pond, and the lungwort's in bloom. |

Vova does not respond.

PROKHOROV: Really, why not let the man go to his
               village? After all, he's been asking, ask-
               ing every day, and they've refused every
               time. And now a man has pined away for
               his forested expanses.

GUREVICH: May he rest in peace.

*The four stop while "The Ancient Linden" keeps playing, and
they drink to his eternal rest.*

PROKHOROV: (*staring at Gurevich*) How is this going to
               end, then? All these victories we've had
               over the plague-infested world?

GUREVICH: Oh! Naturally, at first the Russian nation
               will feel happy and triumphant. As if
               in the bosom of the Antichrist. After-
               ward, though, after catching all the af-
               flictions of the vanquished, they'll start
               falling into decay, nothing will remain of
               their former giantness, and they'll scat-
               ter like dust over the face of the earth. Or
               rather, they'll be carried—by monsoons
               from Jaffa—they'll be carried farther
               and farther north, toward the lifeless ex-
               panses, farther and farther north, where
               the days are even cloudier, even shorter,
               which makes dying even more painless
               and trouble-free. Francesco Petrarch.
               Now, while the Russians are flying into
               their very own abyss, the people of
               Jehovah—

PROKHOROV: At last! The people of Jehovah! Alyokha

	and I have already taken up pro-Israel positions. That is, the only sensible ones. That is, first even knocking the Israelis themselves out of those positions!
GUREVICH:	Wow! Bahrain, Kuwait, and the Emirates—obviously, they'll doom us to an oil shortage.
PROKHOROV:	But by that time they won't exist: not Bahrain and not Kuwait.
GUREVICH:	So, and what if they don't? You don't know the Arabs very well. Even when they themselves are gone, their persistent fanaticism and muddleheadedness will live on. So they're going to doom us to an oil shortage. Not that we give a damn. What do we need that oil for anyway? Do you need it, Vitya?
VITYA:	I spit on it.
GUREVICH:	Vitya doesn't even need it. We'll find a substitute for it, that rotten oil. Vermouth, for instance. Right, Kolya?

Kolya continues to weep, more and more softly, and makes no reply. "The Ancient Linden" goes on.

| | So, I will lead you down the path of thunder and dreams! David's six-pointed star will be our fateful guide! They say the star of Solomon's dissolute son had five points. That doesn't work for us, Solomon Davidych, having eight hundred concubines and— |

PROKHOROV:	You are one sorry fucking excuse for a human being: a five-pointed star!
GUREVICH:	(*becoming increasingly animated*) Long live Eretz Israel all the way to the Euphrates.
PROKHOROV:	The Nile to the Euphrates! Is that all?
GUREVICH:	The Nile to the Euphrates! Why think small? It's all well and good, but jump that wall, From the Euphrates go eastward, east— To the Nile at the very least!
ALYOKHA:	From the Sinai to the Kola Peninsula!
GUREVICH:	If anyone looks at us cross-eyed—if there's anyone left to look at us cross-eyed—it will be like in the Talmud: Ben Zoma looked and lost his mind. Ben Azai looked and died. May Providence turn them into ashes! And may the Lord God sweep them away with his broom! So, let's drink to the union of hearts that obey the highest destiny!
PROKHOROV:	To the union of hearts that links Russia and Israel!
GUREVICH:	To Romain Rolland's health! Now I remember why I thought of drinking to that bald devil. Yes, yes, I remember. "And if there were in all of Israel just one righteous man, I'm telling you, you

would not have the right to judge all of Israel!" Rolland, letter to Verhaeren. And the capital of the world would be — what do you think? Jerusalem? Definitely not! Cana in Galilee — that's what the capital of the world would be! Hah!

ALYOKHA: (*in a deep voice*) And you would be-e-e capital of the wo-o-orld. (*Sinks to his cot before finishing.*)

GUREVICH: Our wings would span your whole world, Emmanuel! Don't deprive your-self of predawn feelings! Where is your trumpet, Timofei Dokshizer, the Soviet Union's best trumpeter? Pipe all hands on deck! Another glass all 'round! To the solar plexus of circumstances!

ALYOKHA: (*in a lowered, raspy voice*) Hurrah.

Vitya takes a drink and sinks to the cot, too, beside Alyokha. He's starting to vomit uncontrollably, vomiting even chess pawns and dominoes. Shaken by the vomiting, he makes a few convulsive move-ments with his legs — and falls to the bed, breathless. Gurevich and Prokhorov look at each other enigmatically. The light in the ward starts to flicker. No one knows why.

STASIK: (*rises from his knees and runs by for the last time*) What's the matter, people? Who's first and who's last in line for the Toktogul power station? Why are the Golden Beaches of Absheron so de-serted? Who did I plant flowers for? Why? In 1970, why didn't UNESCO mark the two thousand years since the demise of Queen Cleopatra of Egypt?

He falls silent again, this time with a bowed head and his hands crossed over his chest, à la Bonaparte on the eve of his final Waterloo, and stays that way until the incursion of medical staff coming up in a few minutes.

PROKHOROV: Alyokha!

ALYOKHA: (*breathing hard*) Yes, here I am.

PROKHOROV: (*pestering*) Alyokha!

ALYOKHA: Yes, here I am. Farewell, Mama. Your daughter Lyubka is leaving us for the damp earth. (*Throws his head back and wheezes.*) My ashes—sprinkle them on the Ganges. (*The wheezing breaks off.*)

PROKHOROV: What is this? Hey, Gurevich, I'm having trouble seeing. What about you? Are you okay? (*Glowering now.*)

GUREVICH: Yeah, I can see okay. The ward's just gotten darker. And it's harder and harder to breathe. You realize I noticed immediately that what we were guzzling was slightly off.

PROKHOROV: Me, too. I noticed almost immediately. But if you noticed immediately, why didn't you say something? Why did you make us drink?

GUREVICH: Who made anyone drink? I just thought—

PROKHOROV: Thought what? And when half the ward had already crapped out, you still just thought? (*Angrily.*) That was your

	intention. Your intention. You always have to have an intention.
GUREVICH:	Yes, I did. My intention was to bring lonely people together. To make peace between those who bear malice, and acquaint them with the little joys, to bring dawn to the twilight of these souls, which were behind bars in here to the end of their days. I had no other intention.
PROKHOROV:	You're lying, you creep. Lying. I know what your intention was. Dispatch everyone to the next world, to their ruin. I saw through you from the very start. René Descartes. Lousy shit.

Makes an attempt to get up off the bed and then, with arms spread wide, advances on Gurevich, who is sitting quietly. But he doesn't have the strength to throw Gurevich down onto the bed.

	Lousy stinking shit.
GUREVICH:	A little more dignity, monitor. Why bring this up now? It's too late. After Vova's death I realized it was too late. We had no other choice but to carry on. As for noticing, I noticed immediately. But I wasn't convinced until it was too late.
PROKHOROV:	Just tell me, the fatal dose — are we already past that?
GUREVICH:	Yes, I think so. Long ago.

They exchange looks full of bottomless meaning. It gets darker and darker.

PROKHOROV:	That means we're fucked. Well, then, there's still a little splash on the bottom there. Hey, forgive me for spitting on you a little in my fit of temper. It's not your fault. Pour what's left, Gurevich. Go halves? Ready?
GUREVICH:	(*perfectly calmly*) Yes. Only dying here is against nature. Between steep riverbanks? Sure. Between tall rows of grain? Anytime. But here!

They clink mugs. Their breath is coming a little harder than before.

Anyway—first I have something important to do, one promised visit.

Prokhorov, clutching his throat and heart, is slowly bending toward the pillow.

(*hammering away mechanically*) They're Maying it over there. They have champagne pouring, and sterlets. They're good and high, and we're like samurai. They're aerials; we're burials. But we're in it for the long haul. We'll get up any minute now. That freak of nature with her? Really? A few hours already—with her? But I was talking about Cana of Galilee. "Gurevich, dear man, everything's going to be fine." That's what she said. Now we'll see just how fine everything's going to be. Right away, right away.

Jumps up and collapses back into his chair.
Backstage—or coming from inside the walls—a decadent song by

Nadezhda Obukhova: "Oh, dear night, you dear dark, dark night."
Etc.

You invited me to dinner, Goon, so here
I am, for breakfast. The wonderwork-
ing tart! Natalie! While I'm sitting there
acquiring modal inflections, they're —
Lord, don't torture me — meanwhile
they're —

Lets his head fall on the nightstand and clutches his hair.

VOICE FROM ABOVE: (*a voice that has more the metal of a cold
than any imperative in it*) Vladimir Ser-
geich! Vladimir Sergeich! Get to work,
work, work. Go get fucked, fucked,
fucked.

GUREVICH: (*raises his head and looks at the bird with
immeasurable bafflement*) Merciful God!
What is this? I can barely see. Give me a
Bible and a staff — and a little guide. For
a small donation I'll travel the world and
spread the word. Now I know what to
spread the word about.

VOICE FROM ABOVE: Vladi-mir Sergeich! Vladimir Sergeich!
Get to work, work, work. (*Faster.*) Go get
fucked, fucked, fucked.

*Gurevich with great difficulty rises slightly from his chair, cling-
ing to the nightstand for all he's worth — trying, trying not to fall.*

GUREVICH: While I still have at least a little vision
left, I'll get to you, I'll come to breakfast.
B-brute.

Steps away from the nightstand. Sways and takes a first step, and a second.

It's okay. I'll get there.

A third step. A fourth. Tripping in the dark over the rear admiral's corpse, he falls. Slowly, grabbing onto the back of someone's bed, he rises.

I'll get there. By feel, by feel, little by little. I'll get my hands on that throat eventually. I just can't leave it like this, Natalie.

It's almost pitch-dark. A fifth step. A sixth. A seventh.

God, don't let me go completely blind. Before I have my revenge.

He falls again, cracking his head on the edge of the next bed. Two minutes of loud, helpless, shaking sobs.

I'll get there. I'll crawl there.

How is he going to manage this? He stands up to his full height. Testing the space in front of him with his hands, he takes another five steps—all the way to the doorjamb.

Just a sec. I'll take a breather and then down the hall, along the wall, the wall.

Prokhorov, who has been lying there calmly, raises his head and lets go with a shout that startles all the wards, all the sleeping and not sleeping male and female nurses in the distant doctor's lounge and doctor's office. People don't shout like that in this world. Agitated, half-asleep, and boozed up, everyone on duty, with Raninson in the lead, comes down the lit corridor toward Ward 3 with the tread of Fortinbrases. The first thing they encounter is a barely breathing Gurevich, who is now totally blind and has a blue and bloodied face. Borenka the Goon kicks him clear of the ward door. They all burst in.

RANINSON:	(*shouting over the clamor and hubbub*) Straight to the telephone! Call central and the morgue!
DUTY NURSES:	(*higgledy-piggledy*) But this one! This one died standing! Arms crossed! He still hasn't fallen; he's leaning against the wall. The entire methyl reserves— cleaned out! No, there's one still breathing, I think. Who shouted like that? (*And so on. And so forth.*)
A HEAP OF ORDERLIES:	(*fat, with stretchers*) I can't remember ever having a crop like this.

The removal of the dead begins, one by one. End of the finale of Sibelius's Second Symphony.

BORENKA:	Natasha, where are your keys?
NATALIE:	(*beside herself, isn't even crying*) Oh, I don't know. I don't know anything.
ONE OF THE NURSES:	But Kolya, why did they carry out Kolya! He's still breathing a little.
RANINSON:	(*venomously*) It's all right! To the morgue with him, too! The autopsy will show whether we're dealing with clinical death or clinical imbecility!
BORENKA:	(*lifting Gurevich's wounded head with his foot*) What about this? What do we do with this?

RANINSON: Watch him. I'm going to the telephone.
                        I've got my hands full making calls.

*Borenka drags Gurevich by the legs to the middle of the ward.
Neither the blind man nor the audience can see anything. Borenka
can see everything.*

BORENKA: Well, how're we doing, worm? Longing
                        for the crematorium? Your stinking tribe!

Several kicks to the side and head with his heavy boot.

                        The crematoriums weren't enough for
                        you! You poisoned everyone, you know,
                        you Jewish shit. Everyone!

GUREVICH: (*raspily*) I-I knew nothing.

Another blow.

                        I'm blind. I can't see anything.

A blow.

NATALIE: (*out of the dark*) What's going to happen
                        now? What's going to happen now?
                        Mama! (*Staccato sobs. Weeps like a
                        little girl.*)

BORENKA: Blind, you say? You stinking boil! You
                        once lived in Paradise: if someone
                        whacked you in the face, you could see it
                        all. But now—you're going to see fuckall!

*At every one of Borenka's retorts, Sibelius fades away for a while,
and then the music rushes in again, music that, if it were put into
the language of smells, would stink of rotten pork, dog meat, and
burnt fur.*
He gives him another kick, then another in the head.

NATALIE: (*hysterically*) Borka! Stop it! Stop it! This is insane! Stop it already! (*Descends into cascading sobs.*)

BORENKA: (*with mounting frenzy*) There should be gas chambers built for all you pigs!

Several kicks to the kidneys: the blind man's snarling and the male nurse is puffing.

Festering fag! Fucking beast! Dirtbag!

The curtain is closed now and could open, as a matter of fact. But there, behind the curtain, the action continues just the same, and without mercy. Gurevich's roaring grows increasingly deadly. A sack of sheets comes flying out at the audience from the ward, through the curtain; it's followed by the nightstand, which shatters to pieces. Then by the cage with the parrot, already dead from it all.

No applause.

TINY EPILOGUE

"Music before all else" — without that it's impossible. Other than the author's indications already strewn through the text, you can (very quietly) use Russian folk songs like "The Pathways Have Grown Up" and "On the Road to Murom" — preferably orchestral variations on these themes (in Act 3). The Russian song "By the Dawn, the Lovely Dawn" (in the first half of Act 4). Part one of Mahler's Third Symphony, very subdued, in Act 1. Something from the most measured and dreary parts of Bruckner's Andante in Act 5. Well, and so forth . . .

VENEDIKT EROFEEV (1938–1990) was among the most prominent writers of the Soviet underground culture and Russian postmodernism. His prose poem *Moscow to the End of the Line* has been translated into many languages and has earned Erofeev international acclaim and cult literary status.

MARIAN SCHWARTZ is a prize-winning translator of Russian fiction, history, biography, criticism, and fine art. She is the principal English translator of the works of Nina Berberova, as well as the translator of the *New York Times* bestseller *The Last Tsar*, by Edvard Radzinsky, classics by Mikhail Bulgakov, Ivan Goncharov, Yuri Olesha, and Mikhail Lermontov, and fiction by contemporary writers such as Olga Slavnikova, Andrei Gelasimov, and Mikhail Shishkin.